Stirling thrust himself [...] of the lid bowed u[...] snapped flat again, thr[...] knees. He swore furiously. So that was it. [...] had secured the lid intending Stirling to remain in the container until it reached the blades. Or would it be crushers?

Growling with effort, he drove up again with bunched shoulders. The plastic ruptured into sharp-edged tongues which tore into his skin as he went through.

As he struggled to extract his legs from the obstinately contracting hole in the lid, Stirling caught a glimpse of sterile blue sky patterned by overhead girders, a green horizon on his left, and his immediate predecessors in the line of yellow containers. They were jostling along a roller way and over a line of snarling circular blades which ripped them open from underneath, allowing the white powder to fall through into a hopper. There were less than five seconds to go before he reached the ripsaws, and his ankles and feet were still enmeshed in the tough triangles of plastic.

# BOB SHAW

## THE SHADOW OF HEAVEN

VGSF

VGSF is an imprint of Victor Gollancz Ltd
14 Henrietta Street, London WC2E 8QJ

First published in Great Britain
in 1978 by Corgi Books

This revised edition first published in 1991
by Victor Gollancz Ltd

First VGSF edition 1992

Copyright © 1969, 1991 by Bob Shaw

A catalogue record of this book
is available from the British Library

ISBN 0 575 05294 5

Printed and bound in Great Britain by
Cox & Wyman Ltd, Reading

# Chapter One

Stirling's first story of the day was a routine job. The bodies of a young man and woman, handcuffed together, had been dragged out of the Merrimack during the night. The piece was worth two or three paragraphs as it stood, more when he had established *who* and *why* – but nothing was working out to his satisfaction that morning.

His best contacts at police control and the morgue were off for the day, and his second-best contacts really were second-best – probably because they were getting better sweeteners from broadcasters and other newspapers. Stirling had wasted thirty minutes on futile phone calls when one of the *Record*'s government-sponsored student reporters dropped a note from the news editor, Sam McLeod, onto his desk. McLeod was a gloomy little man who, in a lifetime in the news business, had had a million print-outs through his hands, yet never failed to summon up a fresh look of savage hatred for each new sheet that was handed to him. He sat within five metres of Stirling and the other city reporters, but – in what some thought was an attempt to associate himself with historic editors – always communicated by means of handwritten notes. This one said:

"What's the holdup on the John and Jane Doe story?"

Stirling swore savagely and called up a new document on his computer terminal. "Tell Sam I'm gummed up on this one. I'm putting through a holding story for the noon edition." He glanced up at the trainee and sniffed. "Nice perfume, Jean. Smells expensive. What is it?"

Jean smiled, highlights moving on her fashionably pearlised skin. "It's called Roast Beef."

Stirling sniffed again, even more appreciatively, because he could remember having smelled real roast beef when he was a boy. "Don't come any closer or I might try to eat you all up."

"Is that a promise?" Jean winked at him and stalked away on invisible, paramagnetic high heels which made her look as though she was walking on tiptoes as she moved down the long room. Huge oblong prisms of morning sunlight sloped from the side windows, picked out columns of cigarette smoke and occasionally exploded silently over white-shirted figures.

Looking after the young woman, Stirling was once more impressed by the spaciousness of the *Record*'s editorial offices. The room was about 35 metres by 15 metres and housed a staff of 200 – which meant that each member of the editorial team had enough room for a knee-hole desk and a swing-out stool. He guessed that the area would have seemed impossibly cramped a century ago, but when he compared it to the stifling claustrophobia of his apartment he felt like staying in the office till bedtime. He had actually tried that a few times, but when the place emptied at night it began to seem *too* big. At those times he was glad to have been born after the Compression, and not before.

Stirling wrote two single-sentence paragraphs giving the facts he had, took off a copy and carried the gossamer-thin but opaque sheet to the news desk. McLeod stared at it in professional disgust.

"Is that it? Is that one hour's output for a supposedly senior and experienced reporter on the *Record*?" He buried his face in his hands and sat waiting for an answer.

"I can't make the stuff up, Sam. That's all I've been able to get so far."

"Have you run any kind of meat scan?" McLeod's voice was blurred as it filtered through his fingers.

"We haven't got the names," Stirling said patiently. "We file people under their names, and when we have no names we can't check the files. It's an inherent flaw in the system, Sam."

"Don't try to be smart with me, Victor." McLeod raised his

slightly yellowed eyes and stared at a point on Stirling's collar. "Have you run through the latest missing-persons files?"

Stirling felt his grip on his temper begin to slide a little. "Well, you see, Sam – there's this name business again. I hate to bring it up since it seems to bother you, but missing persons are indexed by name as well. Names are really catching on, you know. Nearly everybody has one now."

An unexpectedly angelic smile spread over McLeod's face, and Stirling knew the little man was going to score a point.

"I know that, Victor. And they're *cross*-indexed as well. If two people who are connected in some way disappear, it shows in our files. Doesn't it? You just might get a lead on the identities that way, Victor. That's why the *Record* goes to the expense of subscribing to the police data service. Have you done a search from that angle?"

"Of course, I have," Stirling lied. "But I'll do a re-run, if you want."

"That's my boy," McLeod murmured. "We'll make a reporter of you yet." He raised a floral-imprinted cup of synthejuice to his lips and stared over the rim with jaundiced eyes as Stirling threaded his way back to his desk.

Stirling checked himself from swearing as he squeezed his large and rather overweight body through the crowded aisles. He treated swearing as being like antibiotics – indiscriminate use produced a tolerance which left the patient stranded when a real emergency cropped up. And he had a feeling he was going to need some reserves before the day was over.

Technically speaking, McLeod was right about the meat scan, which was trade jargon for looking into the database which was supposed to show up connections between two or more missing persons. In theory the system should have been a boon for serious investigators, but in most cases data were entered only when the missing persons were related to each other, worked for the same business, or were joint members of leisure organisations. Legal obligations for data to be recorded were hardly ever enforced. Stirling had not bothered to run any searches because his instincts told him that the only connection between the two pitiful human shells taken from the river was that they had once looked on each other with love.

In spite of the intense conditioning, some people still wanted to set up house together and bring up their children together – the way it had been before the Compression – and they were not prepared to settle for anything less. Such feelings were not recognised by artificial intelligences – so Stirling had not run any checks. He had to admit, however, that John and Jane Doe might have met each other while working in the same office or factory, in which case there was a chance of getting something on them.

As the computer went through that week's heavy crop of missing persons, Stirling wondered how anybody's emotions could get so much out of control that they would jump into a river. The choice of method was probably significant. Just as the ancient Roman aristocracy had regarded it as a privilege to run onto their swords when they found circumstances intolerable, so a citizen of the twenty-first century could slip quietly away from life peacefully, almost pleasantly, with the aid of a handful of pills. And hardly anyone would notice his departure. But this couple must have wanted to make a protest – and so they had done it the old-fashioned way, the hard way – choking as the black, stinking waters slopped into their mouths and invaded their lungs.

*The fools*, Stirling thought, angry at himself for getting involved even to this extent. All their big dramatic protest was going to get them was a few column centimetres on a middle page of that day's *Record*. Less than that if he failed to get a lead on their identities before McLeod handed him a bigger story.

As the computer scrolled through the names it was trying to pair, Stirling gazed absent-mindedly at the screen. The undistinguished names slid up the smooth glass and vanished, like souls rising to heaven, each representing an undistinguished life, or death. Feeling himself sink further into depression, Stirling turned away from the machine. As he did so, one of the names registered, belatedly, on the part of his mind that was always alert for such things.

*John Considine.*

My mother is called Considine now, he thought mechanically. And my half-brother is called John – but this could not be what it seems. Considine is a common enough name; besides, somebody would have been in touch with me. He hesitated for a moment then went after the name, froze it and called up all relevant details.

The entry was four days old, and it contained very little information. John Considine, aged 31, unemployed mathematician, reported missing by family, no criminal record, no reason to suspect foul play. Stirling skipped the vague physical description, education and employment records, and read the address: Fam-apt 126–46, Flat-block 353, Res-area 93N–54W. When Johnny and he were boys they had joked about that string of numerals and butchered words. (It isn't much, but we call it home. I always think a good address is *so* important, don't you?) Now they served to confirm that the missing person was a flesh and blood reality, not just a collection of glowing symbols on a screen, but the only human being Stirling had ever really known.

He worked his way back to his desk, lifted a phone and keyed in his mother's number. The fluffy calling tone dragged on for a couple of minutes before he accepted there was going to be no reply. Stirling set the phone down and began struggling through the restrictive layout of the editorial office to reach the exit.

McLeod looked up in surprise. "Victor?"

"Can't stop. I have to go out."

"I want to talk to you, Victor." McLeod's voice had developed a metallic edge.

"Send me a note. I'll read it when I get back."

Stirling went out through the doorway and thumbed the elevator button, wondering if he was pushing McLeod too far. It was more than a year since a reporter had been sacked from the *Record*, and McLeod never allowed the big axe to get too rusty.

When the elevator had carried him up to the sixth level, Stirling went out onto the street and signalled for a cab. It was a clean, jewel-bright morning in May and – as there was only one street level above the sixth – sunlight was flooding freely over the shuttling traffic. It gave him a feeling of airy warmth.

A cab obligingly slowed down, but at that moment three men in the immaculate white uniforms of Food Technologists emerged from another entrance. The cab speeded up again to pass Stirling and picked up the three Techs.

"Hold it," Stirling shouted angrily. "That's my cab."

He ran a few paces towards the waiting automobile, but the men got in and were whisked away. One of them was grinning as he glanced back. Halting his ungainly run, Stirling squandered most of the day's ration of swear serum, although he knew the cab driver had only been looking out for his own interest. The Food Techs were flush with money and could be big tippers; they were also flush with power and a complaint from one of them, no matter how groundless, would be enough to deprive a hack of his licence. About once a month Stirling gave up some of his spare time to write feature articles about this sort of occurrence but, not surprisingly, the *Record* never printed them. The East Coast Government kept a pretty tight hold over what appeared in the media – and the Food Technologists kept a pretty tight hold over the Government.

A few minutes later another cab appeared and Stirling got in. When he had given the driver his mother's address, he settled down in the back seat and stared morosely through the bubble's sides at the unfolding vistas of multi-layered cityscape. The cab was skimming along 600 metres above what had once been the smallish manufacturing centre of Newburyport at the mouth of the Merrimack River. Now the original city was buried in the massive East Coast conurbation, which was effectively a single building stretching from above Boston right down to Miami, and which included New York, Philadelphia and Baltimore in its basement layer.

Roughly one-third of the population of the United States had lived there since the Compression.

Stirling tried to visualise the region as it had been in the bright, brave past when the whole country had been available for living space, but his mind balked at the task. In 1996, almost a century ago, World War III had come and gone, and none of the theoreticians had been able to predict the form it would take. It had always been assumed that the Big War would annihilate most of the population and turn the major countries into vast uninhabited areas similar to what they had been in pre-history. That had been the first misconception. Humanity had survived practically unscathed – the only real casualty had been the land itself.

The second mistake had been in the assumption that – if war came – America, Russia and China would fight it out among themselves in one or another of the few simple permutations possible. In the real event, America, Russia and China had found themselves on the same side; and they never did find out for certain who the opposition was. The enemy had assembled his forces, struck, and retired to safety before any of the Big Three discovered the war had started.

The first indications had come when the soil began to die.

Soil sterility occurred in great swathes from coast to coast and removed traditional agriculture from the tally of meaningful human activities in a matter of months. In the beginning, China had seemed a possible culprit because she was suffering slightly less than Russia and the States; but it was quickly established that this was a lucky accident due solely to the fact that her airline services were underdeveloped in comparison to those of the other two powers concerned – for the unknown enemy had used each country's civil aircraft as weapons carriers.

The annihilation of the soil had been accomplished by widespread dissemination of one of the bipyridylium herbicides, paraquat dichloride, modified to protect its characteristic flat molecules from becoming inactivated through interaction with clay minerals. The beauty of the technique – or the ugliness, depending on how one looked at it – was that the modification enabled the chemical entity to perpetuate itself,

11

even in the harshly inimical environment of jet fuel. At some time in the early part of 1996, the herbicide had been introduced into major fuel depots; and the big jets had obligingly dusted whole continents with it as their exhaust trails drifted downwards in gigantic, invisible, rolling clouds of death.

Only massive technological resources had prevented the extinction of the multitudes the soil supported. When it had become apparent that the work of reclaiming the land would take centuries, the big powers turned to the sea for their food. Whole populations had been transferred to the coastal regions, partly so that they could be more efficiently suckled by the mother of all life, mainly because human existence had become too difficult to maintain under the seething ochre blankets of continent-wide dust bowls.

This was the world in which Victor Stirling had grown up. He had never known any other. But that did not prevent him from occasionally feeling nostalgia for a way of life he was scarcely able to comprehend.


"Oh, it's you. What do you want?"

Mrs Mary Considine glanced up briefly, saw her older son for the first time in two years, and returned her eyes, unimpressed, to a bouquet of artificial ferns she was building from a kit. She was a big woman, heavy-boned, with red forearms and slightly thinning brown hair. Her fifty-five years, the last thirty-five of them in Fam-apt 126–46, had left her practically unmarked on the outside. But sometimes, as she looked out of the apartment's single window and down through the clouds drifting in the street canyons below, her eyes were like those of a sniper, sorrowful and yet intent.

"What do I *want*?" Stirling squeezed his way into the living room and closed the door behind him. "What do you mean, what do I want?"

"We don't see much of you these days. Or should I say these years?"

"I've been busy," Stirling said inadequately, aware of his guilt. "Why didn't you send me word about Johnny?"

12

"Didn't know you'd be interested."

"No, mother, don't talk that way. I want to know about Johnny. Have you any idea where he is?"

Mrs Considine gave a sharp laugh. "That'd be a new departure."

Stirling knew she was referring to the fact that his father had vanished after two years of marriage, her second husband after four, and now Johnny was gone. He resisted an irresponsible impulse to point out that she had made a pun. The matter was too serious. There was nothing particularly unusual about men being unable to stand the psychological erosion of family life in the glove-tight box of a fam-apt. But there was no way of telling if they had managed to evade the immigration barriers thrown up against the Big Three by the other – naturally overcrowded – countries of the world, or if they had chosen to exit from life altogether.

He folded a chair down from the wall and sat on it uncomfortably while his mother brewed coffee. As she moved about, her broad, solid figure almost filling the miniature kitchen, she told him that Johnny had left home exactly a week earlier. He had not said good-bye, nor even left a note; but she discovered later that he had taken all his money and a few personal possessions. The police, when she contacted them, had not been noticeably interested.

Although he could not imagine Johnny ever committing suicide, Stirling was relieved to hear about the money and belongings.

"At least," he said as he accepted a cup of the scalding synthetic, "you know he's still alive somewhere."

"Of course, he's alive. The only thing wrong with Johnny is . . . claustrophobia."

Stirling noticed the slight pause before she uttered the near-taboo word. It had taken a lot of psychologists many years to convince people that the Compression was acceptable, if not enjoyable – but they had just about succeeded. The ability, literally, to rub shoulders with one's fellow man all day and then enjoy a sound sleep in a coffin-sized bedroom, had

13

become the most prized of the social virtues. Logically, claustrophobia had taken the place of epilepsy or tuberculosis as a disease which mothers hesitated to acknowledge in their children.

"Did the police give you the impression they'd be able to find him?"

"They gave me the impression they weren't going to look."

"Then I'll have to try." Stirling sipped the black, bitter drink. "Have you no idea where he might be? Nothing at all to go on?"

"All I know is, he went."

Stirling finished the coffee and lit a cigarette. The age difference between him and his half-brother was only four years, but he found it difficult to accept the idea that Johnny had developed into an adult capable of thinking and acting like a grown man. He kept seeing him as the fair-haired, gap-toothed kid with whom he had shared not only the same bed, but the same pillow, during the timeless dream-years of childhood. At night they had lain in the tiny room, imagining they could feel the 700-metre tower rocking in the night winds outside and telling stories about how they would grow up tall some day and go off in search of their fathers. Sometimes they would imagine discovering them at the North Pole or in Africa, but the usual climax to the boyish fantasies was the finding of their fathers in Heaven.

On an impulse, Stirling crossed to the door of his old bedroom and slid it aside. The room was two paces long by one pace wide. The floor space was completely filled by the bed – but it had seemed bigger when they were children. Everything had seemed bigger then. He leaned on the doorframe and smoked thoughtfully, aware that his mother had stopped work on the ferns and was watching him hungrily.

"Do you get enough money?" He asked the question to discharge the emotional potential that was building up.

"Yes. I've a production contract for these ferns and flowers. Then there's the money you send me, and with what Johnny gave in I was even able to save."

14

"That's good."

Stirling's gaze roved the walls of the bedroom, taking in the miniature pennants and the old photographs. In the centre of the end wall was an empty hook above a brighter patch of colour of the sort that is left when a picture has been removed, but irregular in shape. He tried for a moment to remember what had hung there; then he began to feel the first gentle stirrings of alarm.

"Mother, what happened to Dad Considine's boots?"

"Aren't they still in there? I don't know. They were there till a few days ago. Johnny must have taken them with him."

"But they were fur-lined flying boots. He wouldn't want to wear something like that, for God's sake."

"What's the matter, Victor? Did you want those boots yourself?"

Shaking his head slowly, Stirling sank down onto the edge of the bed and sat staring across the apartment towards the single window. The old, crinkled, leather boots had been the most tangible souvenir Johnny's father had left him; but they had played another, and very important, role in both their childhoods. Having grown up in the Compression they had never been able to visualise clearly what it would be like up in Heaven; but they had been pretty sure it would be cold, and it was agreed that they would wear big boots when they went there to find their fathers. And now Johnny had vanished and taken the boots with him.

Stirling narrowed his eyes against the mid-morning sunlight, focusing them into the eastern sky. He was almost 700 metres above sea level; but four kilometres further up he could just discern the pale silhouette of Heaven, drifting in the thin air high above the Atlantic – cold, serene and utterly remote.

15

## Chapter Two

Stirling lounged in the soft warmth of the space cruiser's control chair. He adjusted the view screen's filters so that space appeared the colour of summer skies on Earth; and far ahead was the slowly expanding disc of Saturn, a spot of creamy light in the gentle blueness. He moved a finger; and, in response to his command, the music that had been whispering around him swelled in dreamy, intangible billows. Silver-sad voices mingled with the drifting chords, creating laceworks of memory, evoking old and almost forgotten thoughts of other times and other places – of the twinkling and tumbling flight of butterflies in orchard shadows, of raindrops patterning the surface of dim lakes. Each impact creating a transient crystal crown.

As Saturn bloomed in the view screen and unfolded its misty rings, Stirling eased the cruiser into a near-perfect circular orbit over the poles. He relaxed again, giving his mind up to the music, and let time itself recede into pictorial abstractions like triangular green flashes strung on a starry helix, every sixtieth one ruby red. This was good. This was living as no one had ever done it before – except that, somewhere far back in his consciousness, was one splinter of worry which seemed to be driving itself deeper and deeper. He ignored it, overlaying the tiny wound with soothing balms of womb-comfort generated by the warmth of the cruiser's control room, the gyrating star meadows in the view screen, and the pulsing nostalgia of the music.

On Stirling's eighth orbit of the planet, his eyes detected a flicker of movement ahead and slightly below his own course. Another ship. He had been watching the mote of light for

16

several minutes before he realised the other pilot was matching velocities and closing in on him. Stirling sighed; he had not wanted company. His cruiser lifted its nose, as he manipulated the sensor-stick, and arced up and away from the plane of the ecliptic. He brought it out of the lazy curve, centred the destination cross-hairs on the distant billiance of Sol, and increased his speed. Relaxing again as the cruiser slid down the long gravity gradient to the sun, he tried to get back into the music but something had changed. A point of light adjusted its position slightly against the star fields in the aft screen, and he knew the other ship was following him. It must be a joy-rider! Stirling instinctively demanded full speed and, tense with annoyance, watched the disc of Sol flower in his screen while the other ship jockeyed for position behind him. He waited until the last possible second, then threw on maximum lateral acceleration. The flaming disc shifted to one side, almost too late; and for three nightmarish seconds he was skimming over boiling hell-scapes while the garish palm trees of solar flares reared up ahead. When the sun had reluctantly dropped away beneath, Stirling looked around and saw no sign of the other ship. It must have gone in. He began to laugh, and the sound was vastly unreal in his ears.

*What am I doing?* I'm supposed to be looking for Johnny.

With a surge of revulsion Stirling released the sensor-stick and immediately found himself sprawled in the padded chair of a cosmodrome. He was sweating under the face mask and earphones. He snatched off the mask and released himself from its hallucinogenic breath. The dimness of the circular theatre was alive with the moans and sighs of the occupants of the seriate chairs. Overhead, filling the auditorium, a huge model of the Solar System drifted in its anti-grav field, while bead-sized spaceships – one for each patron of the cosmodrome – flitted invisibly among the glowing orbs.

Stirling looked at his watch. He had spent nearly an hour in the dream continuum inhaling drugs, radio-guiding a plastic pellet among the shimmering spheres, seeing through the pin-point lenses of its eyes. Angry at the waste of time, he

17

stood up and moved along the aisle towards an exit; he was uncomfortably aware that he had overestimated himself when he decided to pass a few minutes clinically observing the cosmodrome techniques. He had been sucked in and it had been so *real* that his knees still felt weak. An indication of how much muscle tone he had lost during the trip.

At the exit he paused in front of a bored-looking attendant, who was monitoring the sensor-stick outputs at a low console.

"You still have ten minutes," the attendant said, looking up.

"I know. I decided to skip it." Hearing the surprise in the man's voice, Stirling felt a little better. It must have been unusual for anyone to emerge before the monitoring system threw the switches on him.

"Well, was anything wrong with the trip? Your signals were coming through on both . . ."

"Nothing wrong," Stirling interrupted. "I'm looking for somebody. Has Lou Grossmann come on duty yet?"

"Yeah. I think he came in a while ago. He works in the ops level – right at the top of the house."

"Thanks." Stirling went up the stairs on rubbery legs and passed through double doors onto a wide gallery which encircled the auditorium. The spheres of the model planetary system slowly gyrated below the level of the handrail; and here and there groups of technicians worked at equipment banks while others peered over the edge through long-range microscopes. At this level the central sun was unbearably brilliant; and Stirling realised much of its light was screened off from the lower reaches of the theatre where the patrons gorged on twilight illusions. Several of the technicians glanced curiously at Stirling as he moved along the gallery; but years as a reporter had taught him how to project an air of disinterested confidence when invading private premises, and no one questioned his presence. He found Lou Grossmann leaning on the handrail and sipping coffee.

"Hello, Lou."

Grossmann turned, pushed his sunglasses onto his freckled forehead, and looked up at Stirling without recognition for a few seconds.

"Victor Stirling," he finally said. "What are you doing here? I thought you were on the West Coast."

"No. I've been busy lately and haven't had much chance to visit the family." Stirling hesitated, wondering if Grossmann knew about Johnny's disappearance. "This is the first time I've seen anything like this." He gestured towards the yawning blackness beyond the rail.

"I guess it must be quite a sight the first time," Grossmann said tiredly, "but it's just a job like any other. A joy-rider went right through the sun a few minutes ago. That's the third this week. Disrupts the surface field for an instant and diffuses the gas; then we have to send in a servo-vac to gather it up – which means closing everything down for an hour in case the machine sucks up a couple of ships and scares hell out of the customers." Grossmann smoothed his red hair and gazed at Stirling with frank curiosity.

"I'm trying to find Johnny," Stirling said. "Have you any idea where he is?"

"Sorry. I haven't seen him in three months."

"Oh! My mother said you and Johnny usually had a few beers on Saturdays, and I thought . . ."

"We used to, but he stopped coming round. Like I said, about three months ago."

Stirling nodded and turned away. This was the story he had been getting everywhere. Johnny Considine had never been a steady worker; but since his teens he had been as regular as clockwork in visiting his chosen playgrounds, which were the bars, multi-houses and thrill palaces of First Avenue. Until three months ago, that is, when a change seemed to have come over his life. Was it something to do with his disappearance? Stirling was walking back along the gallery when Grossmann called his name and he turned.

"Johnny's vanished, hasn't he?" The little redhead sounded almost sympathetic.

"I guess so. Yes."

"Mrs Considine worried?"

"What do you think?"

Grossmann looked vaguely guilty. "He's been seen going into that Receders meeting place near the longshoremen's office."

"The Receders!" Stirling's voice was incredulous. "But Johnny's never been to church in his life."

Lou Grossmann shrugged and looked back into the pit, where shadow worlds rolled their slow courses and the minds of men flitted among them like gnats on the surface of a pond. It was obvious he was sorry he had said as much as he had, and suddenly Stirling realised he had just been given his first real lead in two weeks of searching. He muttered his thanks, went down to the street, and was slightly shocked to discover there was still daylight outside. The visit to the cosmodrome had taken only an hour, but it seemed much longer.

At the nearest corner he waited a few minutes for a taxi, but saw only two, each of which had a white-uniformed Food Tech in the rear seat. Lighting a cigarette, he began walking east towards the harbour area, trying to convince himself he was glad of the exercise. The mid-evening traffic was relatively light, and the lowering sun was bathing the buildings in a warm reddish glow which Stirling found unexpectedly pleasant even though he knew what was causing it. Since the death of the soil, dust storms constantly strode across the country west of the static screens which offered partial protection to the coastal conurbation. The splendid Wagnerian sunsets which resulted were a poor consolation for living on plankton steaks, sea porridge, and the other forms of nutriment wrested from the ocean by the Food Technology Authority. There was always the fresh vegetable food sent down from Heaven, but it had traditionally been rare; and it seemed to Stirling the supplies had been growing even more meagre for several years. As he walked, he searched the segments of eastern sky which could be seen beyond the banked apartment buildings. And finally he found the rose-pale silhouette of Heaven, riding in its serene security high above the Atlantic. He thought he detected a glimmer of movement at one point on its upper edge, but at that distance it was impossible to be certain.

Could Johnny, somehow, have made his way up there?

If a road existed Johnny might have found it. He had always had a reckless, burning discontent with life in the Compression which could have driven him anywhere. Stirling remembered how, as a boy, Johnny Considine had been unable to accept the fact that, although mankind was all dressed up with spaceships, there was nowhere to go. In the context of billions of hungry humans to be transported, established, and fed, the other planets of the Solar System were of about as much value as their gaseous counterparts in the cosmodromes. Later, Johnny had tried all the various arms of the Space Service, but the academic standards had shut him out. By that time Stirling had moved away, seeking his own escape in the world of newspapers; and he had done nothing to prevent his brother's life closing up on itself. Was that why he now had this need to trace Johnny? Was he, belatedly, trying to make amends for his own failings?

Depressed with the rare venture into self-analysis, Stirling stopped pushing his way through the crowds on the sidewalks and began looking for cabs again. He got one on the third attempt and directed the driver to take him to the docks. Getting out near the headquarters of the longshoremen's union, he had to scan the block closely to find the meeting room used by the Receders. It was on the second floor of a shabby sandstone building, above a run-down office-supply store. A photo-printed notice at the foot of the narrow stairs said:

'NEWBURYPORT RECEDERS CHAPEL
Nightly Readings – All Invited.'

Stirling went up the stairs and into a long room filled with people listening to a speaker on a low platform at the far end.

An undulating slab of cigarette smoke hung in the choking air, just below the main ties of the exposed roof trusses. Finding a seat near the back, Stirling covertly examined the people nearest to him.

All he knew about the Receders was what he had gained from stray references in the papers: that they were a religious, semi-left-wing group who seemed to be against just about every feature of present-day life. They had a loose organisation under a shadowy figure called Mason Third, who – according to some rumours Stirling had heard – was supposed to have political aspirations, although his platform had never been defined. Stirling had automatically filed the odd facts away in his reporter's memory, and instinctively had categorised Third as one of the army of religious crackpots who helped fill the news columns during the silly season.

Consequently, he expected to find himself sitting among an assortment of human wrecks, misfits, and mooncalves who made up the bulk of the attendance at dockside missions. Instead, those nearest him seemed to be solid, normal citizens – with a sprinkling of sophomores and housewives thrown in. Several were making notes of the speaker's remarks.

Stirling turned his attention to the platform. The speaker, a conservatively dressed man with white hair and a let-me-be-your-father face, was arguing against enforced birth control by giving a detailed account of the failure of the Chinese Experiment. Stirling, who had thought the experiment was a success, listened closely as the speaker described the difficulties the Beijing government had run into in their massive programme of using oestrogens to make the menstrual cycles of all Chinese women coincide, then forbidding sexual intercourse on a national scale on the maximum fertility days. The experiment, the speaker concluded, was an awesome attempt to bring not only thought but emotion into the sphere of state control, and as such was bound to be rejected.

When the white-haired man went off and was followed by another who discussed the deficiency diseases likely to be brought about by the processed foods issued by the Food

Technology Authority, Stirling began to realise he had completely misjudged the Receders. He had been mistaken in thinking them religion-orientated – but what had caused the mistake? Was it deliberately fostered by the organisation itself? They called their meeting places "chapels", a word which usually had religious connotations; and the name, "Receders," was the essence of harmless negation. It was suggestive of noise abaters, flat-Earthers, and complete abstention societies. Had an expert functional semanticist chosen those words?

Stirling decided to check the organisation's file in the *Record*'s office at the first opportunity and see what he turned up. Probably nothing, but any information at all might be useful at this stage – assuming he was not following a false trail. He glanced around the seedy décor of the room and noted the darkened paintwork, the cluttered notice-boards, the worn floor tiles. What was he supposed to do now? Start buttonholing people and asking if they knew where he could find his brother?

Suddenly aware that it might have been better to think about hiring a private investigator, Stirling began methodically scanning as many faces as he could with the faint hope of recognising someone and perhaps taking things one step further. He barely noticed the appearance of a third speaker, introduced as Duke Bennett, a grey-uniformed man of about fifty, with thick sloping shoulders and slightly bowed legs that suggested a kind of inhuman strength. Stirling was feeling for his cigarettes, and at the same time wishing for a cold beer, when he realised the new speaker was talking about Heaven.

". . . The whole concept of the International Land Extensions was a product of the hysteria which followed in the wake of the events of 1996. But we must not be too contemptuous. The incongruity of the idea is a measure, not of the impracticality of the people who built the Iles, but of their desperation.

"After all, any legislative body would have to be in a pretty bad way before it would approve the expenditure required to build huge rafts, boost them five kilometres into the sky, and import tons of soil to cover them – simply to produce a few mustard greens!"

The speaker paused to allow several of the audience to titter appreciatively, then continued in his overloud voice, which hurled the words out like metal ingots.

"We can forgive the builders of the Iles, but we cannot – on any grounds – justify them. The maintenance of the anti-gravity units alone uses up enough hard cash each year to finance the reclamation of hundreds of square kilometres of prairie. In terms of this nation's long range programme, this means . . ."

Stirling, recognising the familiar argumentative patterns, let his attention wander. He could appreciate intellectually that the Iles were not a sound investment, but his emotional response was a different story altogether. It had been a wonderful thing for two fatherless boys, born into a world where magic was less than a memory, to be able to look into the sky and actually *see* Heaven; to share the same cramped bed in a boxlike room; and to feel at peace because up there, high in the east where they could look at it, was that ethereal yet tangible Avalon to which they would both find their way and, someday, join hands with the half-forgotten giants who had been their fathers. And in the long nights they had sometimes seen minute, transient flickers of light which might have been signals.

Stirling, the adult, could look back with some amusement at Stirling the child; yet Heaven had never quite lost its aura, even though the mysteries of its name, nature, and purpose were long vanished from his mind. Its official designation was International Land Extension, US 23; but in the fam-apts and dormitories in its shadow it was known, simply, as Heaven. The name was left over from the early days of the Compression when that Ile's open green spaces were tantalising reminders of the past. Nobody lived *on* Heaven, or on any of the other Iles, largely because the government psychologists had made it clear they could make life in the Compression seem acceptable only if *everybody* was in it together. So the thin clean air of Heaven, high above the winds that carried the herbicidal dusts, was reserved for the agricultural robots which tilled its soil.

The flickers of light, which could sometimes be seen on its upper edge, were reflections from polished machine casings or flashes from the welding arcs of the maintenance robots. Unless, of course, one happened to be a small boy with sombre, searching eyes. In which case they were signals.

A ragged spatter of applause announced to Stirling that the speaker had finished. The audience seemed to know, without being told, that there was nobody to follow. Many of them stood up and immediately began to file out, while others near the front determinedly continued to clap. The uniformed man who had given the talk bowed slightly, looked embarrassed, and gave Stirling the impression he was not a professional speaker. He seemed to have been brought in specially to make a point, like a police sergeant roped into addressing a sewing circle on road safety.

Frowning a little, Stirling tried to remember where he had seen a uniform like that before. He got to his feet, wondered how much he had achieved by coming to the chapel, and was beginning to drift out uncertainly with the crowd, when the speaker turned to leave the platform. A triangular, yellow flash at his shoulder caught the smoky light – and suddenly Stirling was able to place the severe grey uniform. The speaker worked in the freight transfer organisation responsible for operating Jacob's Ladder – the "elevator" connecting Heaven and Earth.

Stirling sat down again. Making a token effort to look small and inconspicuous, he gnawed patiently on a thumbnail while the last of the audience shuffled out past him. In theory, nothing except fertiliser and maintenance spares ever went up in the elevator. But neither could a man vanish as Johnny Considine had done – in theory.

When he was sure nobody was looking at him, Stirling took out a little square case similar to those in which jewellers supply diamond rings. Inside was a silver lapel badge graved with a simple helical design. He put the badge in his buttonhole and snap-fastened onto the back of it a hair-fine wire, which ran down through the lining of his suit to a tiny machine in his left-hand pocket.

The weeks of searching had exhausted his limited capability for gentle, patient probing. He had decided on a frontal attack.

## Chapter Three

Whistling cheerfully, Duke Bennett draped his grey uniform on a hanger and locked it away in a cupboard. On his way out of the changing room, he stopped to look at himself in the slightly yellowed mirror; and what he saw made him smile complacently. At fifty he had lost none of his hard-packed muscularity; and, when he got out of those lousy grey cords and into a decent suit, he looked even better than he had as a young man. The girls seemed to think so anyway, and tonight a couple more of them would get the chance to prove it. As he paused to comb his greying, crinkly hair, Bennett marvelled – as he had done so many times – at the weird mathematics of triadism. Having one woman was good, so having two together ought to be twice as good; but, in fact, the amount of pleasure was boosted into a different order of experience altogether. That was the big pay-off, the triadic bonus, which came as surely as the energy bounty obtained by adding that last pellet of fission-able material.

In a way, he thought, it was getting something for nothing – except that his expenses were high. Still, the racket was going well, specially since he had joined the Receders. The number of fresh contacts had not been as great as he had expected; but the quality was good and his annual take was averaging out at about twice his salary. Not bad going. It showed that a guy with brains could still live well, even if he had never set foot in one of those fancy colleges. Bennett made a minute adjust-ment to the glow-gold clasp at his throat, and went out into the short corridor which led from the changing room to the chapel itself. Passing through the door at the side of the platform, he

27

edged his way across to the central aisle and began walking to the exit. The lights had been dimmed, and he was halfway to the door before he noticed there was someone still in one of the seats at the top of the aisle. The man had obviously been waiting for him, because he stood up as Bennett drew near. Seeing the stranger's size, Bennett instinctively shifted his balance in preparation for trouble; but, as he drew closer, he allowed himself to relax again. The big man had a look of ambling softness which Bennett – triumphant veteran of more short, nasty fights than he cared to remember – immediately identified as belonging to someone who could talk faster than he could move.

"You waiting to see me?" Bennett was impatient to get away, but did not want to risk discouraging a possible prospect.

"You guessed it. First time." The stranger spoke easily, in a deep, unaccented voice, and he smiled as he stared into Bennett's eyes. What, Bennett thought irritably, has this big hunk of jelly got to be so confident about? I'll give him twenty seconds, that's all.

"Well, are you satisfied? Or did you want to talk with me too?"

The stranger's smile became a little wider. "Right again. I *did* want to talk to you."

"So, talk," Bennett said impatiently. "Let's have it."

"I'm Johnny Considine's brother."

The words shocked Bennett; but he instantly saw that they had been intended to jolt him, that the whole conversation had been set up for just that reason. He stared blankly, filled with the comforting awareness that his muscle control had been perfect. Nobody tripped Duke Bennett that easily.

"I got relatives too," he said. "That your only claim to fame? Being somebody's brother?"

"So you never heard of Johnny Considine?" The stranger fingered a silver badge in his lapel and kept on smiling whitely.

"Not as far as I can remember."

28

"Too bad. I'm trying to find him."

"Everybody's looking for something," Bennett said brusquely. He had begun shouldering his way past the other man when he felt himself stopped by a hand on his chest. Bennett looked down at the hand incredulously. This guy is *begging* to be chopped in two, he thought. But that means he doesn't know anything and is pushing me to see what'll happen. And *that* means I can't let anything happen. Which is a pity, because I never met anybody so much in need of a stomachful of his own teeth.

"I heard my brother was a regular attender at this chapel."

"That doesn't mean I should know him," Bennett said in the most reasonable voice he could muster. "Look. I'm interested in the Receders' movement. So, the local committee asks me to talk about the Iles, and I agree because I like public speaking. But I only come along here once a week, and I don't know anybody except the committee members.

"Is that fair enough? Do you mind if I leave now?" Bennett stared into the other's grey eyes, wondering if he had been too reasonable by acting out of character.

"Of course not," the stranger replied with a contented note in his voice which Bennett found slightly disturbing. "Sorry to have troubled you."

Bennett went down the narrow stairs and out to the street, where he snatched a couple of deep breaths before heading for the First Avenue hunting grounds. The incident had been a minor annoyance; but there was nothing to get alarmed about. That Considine boy had been an ideal candidate for Heaven, and there was no way in the world for anybody to guess where he had gone. All the same, it might be better if he pulled in his horns for a while. He had enough cash in reserve to keep him supplied with the necessities – the *real* necessities – of life for the rest of the year.

Having reached the decision, Bennett allowed himself to relax; and immediately, the chilly, but pleasurable flutterings of anticipation began in his stomach. His mind lost itself in visions of the simple, yet subtle, triadic permutations of skin

29

pigmentation: white, black, and all the warmly sexual spect-
rum that lay between.

The telepolygraph was an expensive instrument to begin with;
and the fact that its use was illegal had boosted the market
price to several times its true value. About half the cost of
manufacture went into the badge-like receptor, which could
pick up encephalographic activity at a distance of several feet
and measure heart rates when its incredibly accurate
range-finder was aimed at areas of skin pulsation. The rest
went into the comparator network and logic circuits, which
operated a thumb vibrator when certain criteria were fulfilled.

In general, the telepolygraph represented a prohibitively
expensive and elaborate method of finding out if a person was
lying; but it had its uses in some professions. Stirling had won
his from another reporter in a particularly abrasive poker
game, but rarely used it in the course of his work. But this time
it had really justified its existence. The vibrator had stung his
thumb like a wasp each time Bennett was questioned about
Johnny. But knowing a person was lying was not exactly the
same as knowing the truth.

Stirling stood uncertainly at the entrance to the Receders'
chapel and watched Bennett's dapper, gymnast's figure blend
with the apparently aimless tides of people surging along the
pavements and spilling onto the street itself. Realising the
other man was not going to flag a taxi, Stirling grunted with
exasperation and breasted the forces of the crowd. In a matter
of seconds his shirt was clinging to his back, and sweat had
bound his trousers to his thighs, making walking difficult. He
stayed a discreet distance behind Bennett and felt faintly
relieved that there was no need for him to catch up. Bennett
seemed to be a true child of the Compression: his neat black-
and-silver head slid effortlessly through the barriers of flesh,
while Stirling laboured grimly in his wake, like a tugboat
following a racing yacht. The irregular strips of sky, which
could be seen among the high-level traffic lanes, had darkened
to a hectic indigo tinged with dusty saffron in the west.

As they neared First Avenue, the commercial buildings gave way to an assortment of eating places, bars, drug-stores, and pleasure houses. Cosmodromes – with their illusions of space, flight and freedom – were popular; but there were many variations on the basic theme. In the so-called "action" houses, anyone could pay his money, climb into a cradle, inhale the hallucigens, and transplant his mind into the cockpit of a centimetre-long military aircraft. With its micro-miniature cameras feeding him sense data through a radio link, he could fly lonely jungle missions, engage in dogfights, or perform aerobatics. Most of the patrons, however, seemed to prefer bombing and strafing the beautifully modelled cities.

Stirling's single visit to the cosmodrome had satisfied his curiosity about the experience; but, as he struggled along behind Bennett, he began to wish for the chance to stop anywhere, just for the chance to breathe in comfort. The redly glowing signs winked at him. *OXYGEN INSIDE. OXY-CONDITIONING HERE. STEP IN AND BREATHE.* Stirling tried to ignore the invitations. The government issued regular assurances that, although the general oxygen level had fallen slightly with the annihilation of vegetation, any effects which might be felt would be purely psychological. Stirling's opinion was that they might be psychological for all the medium-sized, thin, *dry* individuals whose builds he envied every day; but, for him, the effects were real.

Two blocks from the brightest lights, he rationalised that there was little point in following Bennett all over town. The nearest elevator whipped him up two street levels, where he was able to catch a taxi heading south.

After the pressures and accompanying heat of the bottom-level streets, the deserted spaciousness of the *Record*'s editorial offices was almost welcome. Stirling knew from experience that he would be able to appreciate the emptiness for only a few minutes before the uneasiness set in. That's all right, he told himself. In a society where claustrophobia is a sin, agoraphobia must be a virtue. Slinging his jacket across a

table, he crossed the room to the news desk where the two
nightmen for that week sat in extravagant postures of
boredom. Behind them the long room was cool and cavern-
ous, walled with shadows.

"Hi, Vic," Dolan said, brightening up. "I didn't know you
were on tonight."

"I'm not – so you can forget any sneaky ideas of turning the
terminal over to me for the night." Stirling pushed Dolan's
feet off the desk and sat down on the edge. "Tell me, Chris,
what do you know about the Receders?"

"What is there to know? They're just one of those minor
religious cults. Back to nature, or something like that."

The other nightman, Waldo Fitz, took off a pair of 3-D
television glasses and glanced across at Stirling curiously. Fitz
was a surly, thick-set youngster with absolutely no imagination, but with a mind like a computer. He was also a top-flight
newsman.

"Are you on to a story, big fella? We're short of copy for
tomorrow. You could get the page one lead with a speeding
case."

"No," Stirling said cautiously. "Just asking. Is there a story
in the Receders?"

Fitz shrugged. "It's a possibility. The guy who runs that cult
is called Mason Third. His name seems to keep popping up."

"In what connection?"

"Nothing special. Just crops up, that's all." Fitz selected a
different channel on his spectacles. While the little left and
right pictures flickered like imprisoned candle flames, he
relaxed back into his torpor. A thread of reedy music escaped
the earpieces.

Recognising Fitz as a man who never gave anything away,
Stirling was vaguely dissatisfied. He drifted up to his own
desk, sat down, and pulled a stat-vu terminal over to him.
In response to his keyed request, the instrument began
displaying on its screen all the *Record*'s stock cuttings on
the Receders and Mason Third. Stirling was able to skim
through them in less than five minutes and learned practically

nothing. The majority of references to the cult were in articles giving general surveys of religious movements and contented themselves with describing the Receders as an obscure and very minor sect. Third's own file contained a dozen or so clippings taken over the past fifteen years. They conveyed the impression he was a lawyer or a preacher – or both – who had been hovering on the fringes of the political scene without ever committing himself or becoming aligned. His name had appeared, very occasionally, in various contexts on the transport tribunal/citizens' action group level. Once he had been named as co-respondent in an unremarkable divorce case, and another time had been fined for attemped tax evasion. All Stirling could get out of it was the impression of a shadowy, slightly unsavoury figure, who had come from nowhere and was not going anywhere in particular.

Putting aside his newly found interest in the Receders, Stirling keyed in Duke Bennett's name and the few available facts about his background. There was a slight delay while the central installation searched city directories, electoral rolls, and such police files as were open to the *Record*. Finally, the screen flashed a confirmation that Bennett worked in the freight transfer service associated with International Land Extension, US 23. The only other information was his address, a single apartment on the north side, not very far from Stirling's own place.

Stirling memorised the string of figures. Here was another clue, another signpost. He made a fairly good salary as a senior reporter, and it took no less than half of it to buy him the privilege of living and sleeping alone. So how was Bennett financing his apartment on an elevator man's wages?

It was almost two in the morning before Stirling heard footsteps in the access corridor.

He pressed himself back into the shadows of a doorway and held his press card ready in one hand. The steps drew nearer, and Stirling risked a glance along the corridor. A glow-tube in the low ceiling showed Bennett zigzagging towards his

apartment between two Japanese girls, who had their arms
around his waist and who apparently were working hard to
support him. The cold tube-light picked out the silver streaks
in Bennett's hair. His face was flushed, ecstatic; and the girls
were giggling every time a new loss of balance crushed one or
the other of them against the closely spaced walls. They were
surrounded with pastel clouds of visi-perfume, and their heels
gave off flashes of coloured light at the impact of every step. A
fine pair of professional glowworms, Stirling thought irrelev-
antly. He waited until the group was almost level with him,
then stepped out, waving his card briefly.

"All right, girls," he snapped. "I'll want your names in a
minute. Now stand away from that man."

As he had expected, the two hustlers fled instantly, their
rapid steps throwing showers of chemi-luminescence from
their shoes as though they were drawing power from the floor.
Bennett blinked drunkenly after them for a moment; then his
eyes focused on Stirling's face and became opaque with rage
and disbelief.

"You," he gasped. "*You!*"

"That's right – Johnny Considine's brother. I've got a
proposition for you, Bennett."

Stirling spoke quickly in an effort to avoid the violence he
could see building up in the other man's hard-packed shoulders; but the words were useless. Bennett drove forward, both
fists swinging, all traces of his drunkenness apparently gone.
Stirling had a small fraction of a second to note, with relief,
that Bennett was making the mistake of assuming that a
surface layer of fat meant there could be no muscle underneath. He risked a gambit and allowed his 230-pound frame to
absorb a couple of vicious blows from Bennett while he
manoeuvred for the chance to use his right. The gambit came
close to being a disaster, for the punches were delivered with
professional brutality and really hurt; but Bennett was not
taking the trouble to defend himself. Seeing the opening,
Stirling launched a single, massive right, whose lineage could
have been traced back to the lead-gloved deathblows of the

Roman arena. Bennett's toughness and experience could not prevent him from being lifted off his feet, doubled around the fist, and dropped on his back several paces along the corridor. He skidded a short distance on the smooth plastic and lay still, making wet, clicking sounds in his throat as he struggled for air.

Concealing a certain amount of awe at his own capabilities, Stirling lit a cigarette and stood staring down at Bennett through a mask of smoke.

"Next time . . ." Bennett's eyes slitted with pain. "Next time . . . you won't be . . . so lucky."

Stirling looked unimpressed. "There isn't going to be a next time, Bennett. I'm a reporter with the *Record* and you smell like headline material to me. Could your business stand the publicity?"

"What business?"

"Your export business, of course." Stirling glanced upwards, significantly. "Perhaps I shouldn't refer to it as exporting, though. You *elevate* things, don't you. Things and . . . people."

"You're crazy."

"All right, Bennett. You can crawl into that highly expensive apartment of yours and wait for tomorrow's *Record*. You'll read about yourself." Stirling walked away, wondering if Bennett would know enough to realise that no editor would go to press with the scanty information he had.

"Hold on a minute," Bennett said desperately. "You were talking about a proposition."

Stirling turned, went back, and helped the smaller man to his feet. In spite of his exultation he could feel an uneasy tightening in his lungs – as though they were already struggling with the cold, thin air of Heaven.

## Chapter Four

The terminal station for International Land Extension, US 23, was an artificial island mounted on stilts 16 kilometres off the coast. Five kilometres above its storage sheds, receiving bays, and administrative area was the western edge of the Ile, which was a rectangular raft measuring 15 by 24 kilometres. In the centre of the island was a bank of six freight elevators which ferried supplies up to the Ile and brought back its produce for shipment to the shore. Each elevator was a simple platform structure fitted with negative-gravity units, automatic docking equipment, and remote guidance facilities which enabled it to be operated from a glass-roofed control block.

Stirling had been on the island once before, with a party of journalists on one of the infrequent press visits organised by the East Coast Government; but now he saw it through new eyes.

At the start of the ten-minute skimmer ride out from Newburyport, the island was a slate-blue hump on the horizon, no different from the other irregularities marking the chain of Food Tech processing stations which skirted most of the coast. It was a crisply sunny afternoon with a fresh westerly breeze, which drove the black-looking water along in neat, regular waves. The processing stations, which could be seen to the north and south, were rimmed with lines of white foam as sharp as the finest brush strokes on an Oriental vase. Stirling picked out a number of the freight skimmers busily shuttling loads of the fish protein, marine protozoa, and sea greens which nourished most of the population. Beyond the line of stations, he saw one of the giant trawlers drifting in as it impassively herded shoals, armies, whole deep-sea kingdoms of fish in its invisible magnetic nets.

Living on shore, Stirling realised, it was easy to forget the awesome scale of the Food Technology Authority's operations, or the simple fact that it stood between the people of the United States and decimation by famine. Looked at in that light, Gordon Hodder and the other members of the FTA hierarchy could almost be forgiven for creating a political machine and systematically filling key governmental posts with their own men. There even were arguments in favour of this from the constitutional point of view. Many political theorists had pointed out that, since the US had been virtually divided by the dust into two separate countries, each with its own administrative setup, the FTA was the one, big, unifying force that remained. The nominally Democratic East Coast Government and the Republican West seemed to be drifting further and further apart, creating a political climate in which Hodder might become the first real President the country had seen in nearly a century.

Stirling was not a political animal; but the idea of a country's ruler having absolute control over its food supplies had negative appeal for him. His objection was so ingrained that he had never felt it necessary to express it in less basic terms.

As the processing stations fell behind, the island ahead began to bulk larger on the horizon. While he watched, a black mote detached itself from the upper surface and began the long climb to Heaven. It brought home to Stirling the enormity of what he was setting out to do. The Ile was a huge, misty trapezium filling most of the eastern sky. Wisps of cloud streamed beneath it – obscuring much of the fine detail of its underside – but at this range he could see the protuberance of the centrally positioned power plant. Smaller booster units dotted the structure in a regular pattern – propagating the field which shielded it from the lethal yearnings of gravitation – and between them ran intricate webworks of lattice girders and secondary beams.

Why, Stirling wondered numbly, why would anyone want to leave the ground and live up there? Green fields and fresh food there might be – but a man would be exposed, with a naked sky above, and five kilometres of windy darkness yawning below his bed while he slept. The idea was . . . *unthinkable*. Suddenly Stirling did not want to go and was unable to produce any reason for going. There was no longer any mystery about Johnny's fate: Bennett had confirmed that he had bought a one-way trip to the Ile. His mother had been hit harder by the disappearance than her despair-moulded nature would let her admit; but what would be solved by dragging Johnny back by the seat of his pants? And if he, Stirling, was being motivated by a belated need to play the role of a protective big brother, was there not some less traumatic gesture he could make to the memory of the flushed, defenceless face that had shared his boyhood pillow?

The questions gnawed steadily into Stirling's resolve as the island loomed up ahead – rearing its masts and gantries into the sky. He moved his shoulders uneasily in the unfamiliar grey uniform and walked across the cargo hold to a spot where Bennett was staring moodily into an empty phosphates container.

"You'd better get in," Bennett said. "We'll be berthing in a couple of minutes."

Stirling hesitated, imagining an uninterrupted arch of throbbing blue sky overhead and five merciless kilometres of thin air beneath his feet. An icy feeling started in his groin and crept upwards in a leisurely tide through his abdomen and stomach. He gripped the edge of the container, crushed the thick buttery plastic, then noticed Bennett staring up at him with open malice.

"What's the matter, big man? Changing your mind?"

"I'm not changing my mind."

"I wouldn't blame you if you did. A guy would need to be sick before he would want to get up on that thing. There's time to call it quits."

"Forget it." Stirling clambered into the container and hunkered down in its base to let Bennett fit the lid.

Bennett shrugged. "All right, big man, but don't make any mistakes. Remember to check your watch as soon as you feel the elevator take off. The trip will take twelve minutes, give or take a few seconds. Then you'll be shunted onto a transfer belt.

"I've kept this container near the end of the batch, so you'll have a good five minutes before it reaches the openers. The blades slice off the top as clean as a whistle . . . So don't be in there too long."

Stirling nodded doggedly.

"We'll give you two minutes from time of arrival – that is, exactly fourteen minutes from the second you take off – then you break out in a hurry. Fourteen minutes, remember. I'll be in the monitoring room down here distracting the duty officer exactly then. But I won't be able to keep his eyes off the screen more than about thirty seconds. You'll have to move real fast. Understand?"

"Wait fourteen minutes and jump out," Stirling said impatiently. "It's hardly as abstruse as anti-grav field theory."

Bennett grinned. "Theory on the ground and practice up there are two different things. You'll see."

Stirling stared at him expressionlessly as Bennett fitted the yellow plastic lid, which shut out all light except for a dim mustard radiance from above. It occurred to him that Bennett might be lying about the sequence of operations up on the Ile and their timing. What if the phosphates containers were shunted off the elevator directly into an opening machine? Or even a crushing machine? After all, the containers were disposable; so there was no need to baby them around. And with Stirling dead there would be little to incriminate Bennett even if the monitoring team glimpsed his body. The guards at the shore checkpoints would hardly remember seeing the two men walk through together.

Negative thinking, Stirling told himself. He could not fully understand the pressures that were driving him up to the Ile in his brother's footsteps; but he knew he was not turning back at this stage. Stirling spent a few minutes going through the small pack which he had prepared, at Bennett's advice, and checking its contents. He had brought a foam-insulated sleeping bag, a supply of individually wrapped protein bars, and a powerful handlight. There was no telling how long it would take to find Johnny and persuade him to return, and he had tried to reconcile himself to the idea of being aloft for several days.

Getting back was a comparatively easy problem, because at this time of the year large daily consignments of lettuce and other leaf vegetables were taking the big drop every day. The cases were loaded out of range of the monitoring cameras; and Bennett had supplied a schedule of his own shift times for the coming week, plus instructions on how to mark the case in which they chose to hide.

Stirling felt the skimmer lurch as it reached the island and went up a ramp into its berth. There was a brief delay followed by a period of jolting and slithering sensations. Indecipherable shouts punctuated the querulous whining of servos, and he wondered just how many strings Bennett was pulling to circumvent the normal weight and irradiation checks which might have revealed his presence.

Crouched in the saffron twilight of the container, Stirling held his watch close to his eyes and waited for the ascent to begin. He wondered if he would be sure of the exact moment.

He was sure.

All anti-grav vehicles designed for passenger transport divert part of the frustrated gravitic force through a field reversal stage, in effect creating an artificial gravity on the upper side of the craft. This was an unnecessary refinement on a vehicle intended purely for freight work: it was cheaper and simpler to ensure that the cargo was either in secured containers or netted in position to prevent it drifting. Stirling's first intimation that the elevator had begun to rise was a sudden feeling that he was falling, hurtling downwards just as fast as the Earth could suck him in. He drifted up from the base of the container, vainly grabbed for an anchor point, and brushed gently against its lid. All the ancient instincts in his body told him to scream because, since the dawn of life, every creature that had ever experienced this sensation was destined to die within seconds.

An indeterminate time went by before cool-fingered logic told him that he could not be falling and that he was merely being screened from the force of gravity. Stirling forced himself to relax, then realised he had not noted the take-off time on his watch. He looked at the jerking sweep-hand – the blind present tapping its way into eternity – and wondered, ten, twenty, thirty, seconds? Settling for twenty, he got his back against a wall of waxy plastic, braced his feet on the opposite one, and waited out the long climb to Heaven.

On reflection, he should have expected the weightlessness. It was that very phenomenon which had been a major factor in halting the spread of the International Land Extensions. In the panic years which followed 1996, money had been no barrier and the Big Three's first impulse had been to create an air-borne agriculture – if necessary, to span seas and oceans with anti-grav rafts. A start had actually been made on such a programme; but the new science of anti-gravities had run foul of man's oldest – astronomy. It became clear that raft construction on the scale proposed would have screened off a sizable proportion of the mutual attraction of Earth and Sun, and would have sent the planet into a widening spiral away from the celestial hearth. A new start was made with Iles in which only the supporting structural grid was screened – a vastly more difficult engineering proposition – but by then the FTA was already getting results from the ocean, and the Ile programme lost way.

Stirling's next indication that the elevator was gaining altitude came when he began to feel the cold, but the drop in temperature was one thing he had expected: even as boys he and Johnny had realised the need for big boots when walking the uplands of Heaven. He slipped the straps of the pack over his shoulders and struggled into a kneeling position, ready to burst through the lid of the container. His watch was showing just over twelve minutes gone when there was an abrupt return of weight and a sense of trundling, lateral movement. A variety of overlapping mechanical sounds filtered through to him: hydraulic moans, the dull thunder of pumps and meshing gears, occasional shrill squeaks.

Stirling's mouth was dry. *I'm five kilometres up in the blue*, he thought, *and there's nothing above or below me. Will I be able to control my arms and legs? And my bladder?*

At exactly fourteen minutes Stirling thrust himself up-wards. The flexible plastic of the lid bowed upwards momentarily, then snapped flat again, throwing him back down on his knees. He swore furiously. So that was it! Bennett had secured the lid intending Stirling to remain in the container until it reached the blades. Or would it be crushers?

Bracing his hands against broad knees, Stirling put his back against the lid and exerted all the lift of which his outsized body was capable. The lid domed upwards, but did not break. *Wait for me, Johnny. For God's sake wait for me!* Growling with effort, he drove up again with bunched shoulders. The plastic ruptured into sharp-edged tongues which tore into his skin as he went through.

As he struggled to extract his legs from the obstinately contracting hole in the lid, Stirling caught a glimpse of sterile blue sky patterned by overhead girders, a green horizon on his left, and his immediate predecessors in the line of yellow containers. They were jostling along a roller way and over a line of snarling circular blades which ripped them open from underneath, allowing the white powder to fall through into a hopper. There were less than five seconds to go before he reached the ripsaws, and his ankles and feet were still enmeshed in the tough triangles of plastic.

Stirling kicked out frantically, feeling cloth and skin give way on the rough edges; then he was tumbling sideways, clear of the train of containers. He leaped from the roller way into the struts of a lattice girder which paralleled it, dropped onto a flat area crisscrossed with metal tracks, and sprinted in the direction of the green horizon. His feet were sliding on a thick

42

coating of frost, and the gelid air ravaged his throat and lungs. To his right, an angular, bright red object whined into life and sped towards him on wheels limned with purple fire.

Reaching the edge of the flat area, Stirling discovered, too late, that he was about five metres above the level of the vegetation he had glimpsed. The red object chattered at him and whipped the air with chromium arms. He jumped blindly out from the edge and smashed down into a world of wet green foliage and black earth. His legs, unprepared for the impact, doubled up and he pitched forward, landing on a smooth rock half buried in the soil.

Incredibly, there was a moment of perfect silence and peace: the red machine seemed to have lost interest in him once he vanished from its precinct. Stirling sat up cautiously, trying to regain his wind, and noticed something unpleasant about the rock on which he had fallen. It was whitish in colour, and had gaping eye sockets.

Gold fillings glittered in two of the teeth.

# Chapter Five

There were no broad meadows in Heaven.

In Stirling's childhood dreams the Ile had been a place of rolling pastures, gentle hills and clear streams – a montage of all the ideal features of a world he had never known. Much later, he had realised that, if the Ile resembled any feature of prewar America, it would probably be a huge market garden; but the boyish visions had persisted, overlaying deduced fact with inherited fantasy.

The Ile was divided into plots of 30 metres, and each plot ran the whole of its 24-kilometre length. Each was tended by an agricultural "robot" – if the word could be applied to a machine resembling a beam crane which straddled the plot and could move along it on metal tracks at speeds up to 80 kilometres an hour. Hanging from the underside of the beam was a room-sized casing which could move laterally to reach any point on the plot. And beneath the casing clustered a tangle of multi-jointed spider legs, tipped with the tools of its trade: spades, nozzles, knives, metal claws. Some of the appendages had eyes.

Stirling had been walking for almost ten minutes before he got his first good look at one of the machines. The sector through which he was moving was planted with coarse beans on both sides – the heavy foliage dappled here and there by white flowers with huge petals like butterfly wings. There was a choking smell of rank *green-ness*; and Stirling, walking in the sunken track bed, found himself passing along a narrow alley of vegetation whose walls were higher than his head. He had never seen anything approaching it, even in underground hydroponics plants. A part of him tried to respond gratefully to the private world of green silences, but who could enjoy solitude?

*I'm alone*. The thought kept hammering at him. *I'm alone, alone, alone*.

Never in his life having been separated from other human beings by more than twenty paces, never having been free of the insensate pressure of walls and ceilings, he discovered completely new levels of pain in merely standing upright and walking when his instincts were to find a dark hole and crawl in. Every sense channel seemed to purvey its own brand of agony. He kept his gaze fixed on his feet and walked slowly, heading for the distant boundary of the Ile where, logic told him, a rebel would hide.

The rails under his feet had been vibrating for several seconds before Stirling realised he was in danger again. He raised his eyes and saw the bright yellow, crab-legged structure of an agricultural robot bearing down on him with the speed of an automobile. He threw himself to one side, and the huge machine swept by with only centimetres to spare, its steel wheels singing viciously on the track. It disappeared in the direction of the transit area with its spider legs drawn up beneath the sentiently revolving turret.

Stirling began walking faster. There had been a strangely purposeful air about the robot's furious rush. It might have been returning to base for new supplies; but – there was no way of telling how sensitive it was about the welfare of its crop – it could have been hurrying to investigate the damage Stirling had done when he leaped into the greenery. He guessed that the robot could keep in touch with sensor units located every few yards and that it was tuned to detect damage by, say, picking up the smell of newly released sap.

And there was that crimson metal demon which had rushed him in such frightening, insane determination to smash him with its arms. What was its function? Stirling got a momentary vision of the red object summoning one of the great agricultural robots, mounting its back, and going hunting for the intruder.

The idea would have been ridiculous if considered in the smugness of the *Record*'s office, but Heaven had been nothing like he had expected, and up here it seemed almost probable. Anything could happen in this world of vivid green and aching blue which had the simplicity of a nursery rhyme landscape – and all the underlying menace.

Thinking it over, Stirling was struck by how little he had known about the Iles. Slightly anachronistic they might be; but the air-borne farms were still an important factor in the country's food supplies, and people were bound to be interested. The absence of adequate feature coverage in all the visual media could only mean that Hodder and his cohorts of faceless men in the FTA were pulling strings for reasons of their own. In view of all the virulently anti-FTA articles he had written, Stirling concluded, it was a little surprising that he had been allowed to continue in the newspaper business at all. It would have been child's play for one of the Authority's puppets in the East Coast administration to have had him removed permanently. The so-called Press Council, set up after 1996 as the government's major propaganda instrument, had absolute control of all communications media; and all its members were, directly or indirectly, FTA nominees. Perhaps, then, the material he had written had not been as good as he had thought at the time.

Stirling scowled as he tried to keep up his speed between the closely spaced tracks. Having his views suppressed was one thing; not even being noticed by the suppressors was another.

There was no way he could estimate how fast he was moving; and, after two hours' steady marching, he felt like a man utterly remote from civilisation and swallowed up in an alien dimension of green life – like an ant crossing a lawn. So far, he had seen nothing growing except beans; but a mental calculation showed him he was moving between only two of the 30-metre strips out of some five hundred similar plots running the length of the Ile. Summoning up all his resolution, he heaved himself up onto the level of the soil bed and looked out across the broad acres. The scene was unexpectedly beautiful.

Stirling had not realised vegetation could assume so many different shades of the one basic colour. The mid-evening sun had moved behind him. Its light washed along ruler-straight strips of green which converged in the distance and ranged from bottle green in colour to near lemon, like the warp of a huge tapestry or the striations in a rare precious stone. Agricultural robots were visible on many of the strips; they flamed with ochrous brilliance in the sunlight and looked less inimical when working quietly at their appointed tasks.

About 400 metres ahead, and slightly to Stirling's right, the flatness of the Ile was broken by a large windowless block. He identified it as the upper side of the central power station which he had seen from the skimmer on the way out from Newburyport. The sight of the station was an uneasy reminder that, right at that moment, clouds were drifting below his feet, that everything he could see was supported on thin air by a mathematical trick – a judo hold which man had put on gravity to turn some of its strength back on itself.

Stirling got down into the more reassuring confines of the track bed and began walking again. At this rate, held back by the ankle-twisting rails, it would be nightfall by the time he reached the far end of the Ile. The cuts on his shoulders and lower legs were stiffening up and becoming painful – another reminder that he had not simply opened a magic door into another dimension. Duke Bennett would have to be dealt with as soon as Stirling had his feet on solid ground again.

He kept going for another hour, then sat down to rest and eat one of the protein tablets from his pack. Through sheer force of conditioning, he had almost finished the dry, sickly compress of marine micro-organisms before realising he could have fresh vegetables with it. Stirling had eaten beans perhaps three times in his whole life, always at Christmas. Filled with a strangely exhilarating sense of breaking every rule in the book, he broke off one of the velvety, still immature pods and slit it open with his thumb. The pale green beans were cool when lifted from the moist, white lining, and they tasted good. He began gathering them in handfuls.

As he ate, Stirling realised he felt quite warm – which was surprising considering that the Ile was five kilometres above the Atlantic. At this height the daytime temperature in summer should have been below freezing. Now that he thought of it, the transit area had been thick with frost, and the air in that region had been painful to breathe. The builders of the Iles must have provided heating elements for the protection of their crops, which meant another detail of the boyhood plans had been wrong. Johnny had not needed Dad Considine's boots, after all.

Stirling began to wonder how Johnny had made out since his arrival in Heaven. He had been aloft for a month now and had had time to establish himself, perhaps with a tent if there was a margin between the end of the soil beds and the outermost edge of the Ile. The concept appalled Stirling. While he and billions of others had been sheltered below in snug herd-warmth, could his kid brother have crouched over the ashes of a cooking fire and stared into the darkness of the Ile with bleak, watchful eyes? What had Bennett said? *A guy would need to be sick.*

Shouldering the pack, Stirling stood up and moved on, suddenly anxious to make contact with his brother as soon as possible. The thought had occurred to him that Johnny could have died on the Ile. Up here a comparatively minor accident or illness could result in a skull bleaching among the green stalks, eye sockets choked up with soil.

Sometime later, Stirling found himself approaching the yellow angularities of another robot. From the distance, it appeared to be stationary; but, when he got close, he saw it was rolling along at a slow walking pace. Several appendages were extended from the turret down into the bean rows on his left. He clambered into the soil bed on his right and hid until the huge machine had inched its way past. If, as he suspected, there was one machine to each plot, he could expect to reach the eastern end of the Ile without any further encounters and without being seen by robot eyes.

It was dusk when he discovered he was nearing the edge. A suggestion of a high wall began to emerge from the gathering darkness ahead, and there seemed to be a considerable open space between it and the ends of the soil beds. Stirling's legs were aching from the long and difficult walk, and he was tired. He began to feel something approaching a childish glee. What a shock Johnny was going to get! If he was camped somewhere along the lateral strip, Stirling was bound to find him shortly; and it would be good – even up here – to sit down with his own brother and talk things over, just as they had done in bed at nights when Heaven was only a shadow in the sky. Stirling suspected that exhaustion, strain, and perhaps a lack of oxygen were playing tricks with his emotional balance; but it *would* be good to see Johnny again, regardless of the circumstances.

He finally reached the end of the 24-kilometre alley of vegetation and stepped out into an open area, which disappeared into the gathering twilight on both sides. The space was a good hundred metres across and was bounded on the eastern side by a high metallic wall, beyond which was the unthinkable. Almost immediately his nostrils picked a strange, heavy smell eddying on the evening breezes – a stench of decay. He looked around hoping to see the orange speck of a fire in the distance.

There was light, but not from a fire.

Ghostly shapes drifted in the air close to the wall, luminescently flickering with cold, purple radiance. Instinctively Stirling took a step backwards, but he was much too late.

A bomb of pain exploded in his head and he fell forward, unable to suppress a mental scream as the five-kilometre well of darkness opened up to receive him.

## Chapter Six

One of the armoured guards laid down his spear and shield, and he approached a projection on the Ile's boundary wall. He caught it and twisted with both hands. The two guards behind Stirling urged him forward, and he realised the hideous truth: there was a door in the wall! Beyond the threshold there would be nothing but clouds and black, hungry air.

He fought grimly, but the men behind him were made of steel. They hurled him against the unlocked door; it gave way, and he reeled through.

There was an explosion of brilliance.

Stirling found himself standing in a rolling green pasture. The pure sunlight of a new morning glittered on its streams, dew-hung trees, and emerald scimitars of grass. Some part of him which had been asleep for a long, long time responded to the scene with grateful recognition – this was Heaven, the *real* Heaven. He heard footsteps nearby and looked around. A tall man with greying hair and a youthful, strangely familiar face was approaching. Stirling hesitated, disbelieving, then he ran forward to clasp the man's outstretched hand.

"Father!"

The man smiled. "I knew you would find me, son. Welcome."

Stirling nodded, unable to speak for the tumult of emotion in his chest; then a cold shadow of dread loomed over him. There was something he had to say. Something terrible.

"Father," he said dully. "I have a brother now."

His father's features seemed to dissolve and flow, reforming in lineaments of bleakness. In his eyes Stirling read anger, accusation – and rejection. Stirling shrank away, but his father caught him by the arms. His fingers locked into the flesh with deadly purpose.

"Take it easy," the voice said. "Take it easy and you won't get hurt."

Stirling opened his eyes. He was lying on the ground and looking up into a night sky in which several needle-sharp stars flew in formation through lacy clouds. Two dark figures loomed over him, and he could feel their hands exploring his body, thieving his pockets. He swore and tried to throw the black shapes aside; but his arms were tied with cords which cut deeply into the muscle and made effective movement impossible.

"I told you to relax," the same voice said. "Don't be stupid."

"He seems clean." The second voice was husky and more kindly. "I think he's a new member."

"What about the uniform?"

"What about it? He wouldn't be the first."

"Well . . . We'll keep him tied up till Jaycee has a look at him."

"You and that Jaycee," the husky one replied scornfully. "You haven't *got* to do what he says, Dix. You know, we gave in to him too easily . . ."

"Yeah? I didn't see *you* trying to stop him, Paddy. Where were you when he was beating Luciano's head in?"

"I'm just saying. That's all."

"Well, if you've finished saying, get this guy to his feet and back to the stockade."

The two men dragged Stirling upright and pushed him into walking. He set off submissively, wondering just how much more hellish it would be possible for Heaven to get. For a second or two, he had been relieved to waken from the strange dream about his father; but this was even worse. His arms were trussed to his sides, he felt sick, and his head was ringing with steady pulses of pain as though somebody was still hitting it. He decided to make sure he could still speak.

"Which one of you two clubbed me back there?"

"I did," said the one called Dix. "What are you planning to do about it?"

"Nothing yet. But I've a good memory for names."

Dix laughed. "Is that a fact?"

"Yes," Stirling said evenly. "Specially when they're attached to sadistic little ticks like you."

Dix rounded on him instantly, but Stirling kept walking, brushing the smaller man into his wake. He tensed, expecting a blow from behind; but Paddy dropped back too, and the two men had a whispered argument. Stirling got time to examine his surroundings. They were walking south along a wide margin between the Ile's boundary wall on the left and the black-looking plots of vegetation on the right. The starlight showed the rails for the agricultural robots running out from the line of the soil beds and most of the way across the open space. Between the rails were tanks and pits of varying sizes, and some of the uncovered tanks were filled with water. From the pits came the stench of decay Stirling had noticed earlier; and, looking ahead down the line, he again saw the insubstantial luminosity swirling in the air above them. Dim memories of school texts stirred in his mind. Rotted organic matter was used for soil enrichment; and in the special circumstances which existed on the Ile the gases emitted could be phosphorescent.

That was one thing explained, but who were the two men who had jumped him? Where were they taking him? Was it possible – the idea shocked Stirling – that there was a group of rebels on the Ile? Men who had opted out of society because they hated the Compression so much that they preferred to spend their lives skulking on the huge raft like rats in a granary? Stirling had to force himself to accept the concept of a man becoming so disgusted with normal life that he would, through choice, live as a savage in the alien, inhuman world of the Ile. After all, his own brother had done it – unless Duke Bennett had tricked him to his death. The half-buried skull was evidence that death was not unknown up here.

His jumbled thoughts were interrupted by the sight of a glimmer of reddish light far ahead. He kept his eye on it as they picked their way along the margin for perhaps another kilometre; and, as he drew nearer, Stirling saw other flecks of orange glowing in the darkness.

"What is this?" He spoke as casually as possible. "How many of you are up here?"

"He doesn't sound like a new member to me," Dix said to his companion as he ignored Stirling's questions.

"We'll see. It's all Jaycee's responsibility now, isn't it?" Paddy still sounded aggrieved; and Stirling realised that, even though the inhabitants of the Ile had shed all ties with society, their little community had internal pressures of its own. They reached the first of the small fires, and he saw figures crouched around the embers. Their faces turned curiously as he went by with his two escorts. The dim light showed low, tent-like structures covered with leaves. Cooking smells drifted around him – richer than the most expensive perfumes – and somewhere in the darkness he heard what was unmistakably a woman's laughter, shocking him with its incongruity. A village, he thought, a complete Stone Age village, supported on anti-gravity units in a world of metal dinosaurs. The idea was incredible, yet it seemed there must be dozens of rebels hiding out on the Ile.

In the centre of the village was a larger structure – composed in part of discarded machine casings – which was almost tall enough to let a man stand up in its doorway.

"Wait here," Dix said. Suddenly respectful, he went to the entrance and tapped gently on a hard surface. "Jaycee," he called into the darkness. "I got somebody here for you to look at. He's wearing a uniform."

There was a movement inside the hut, and Stirling felt stirrings of premonition, a kind of psychic pressure. The man who emerged was as tall as Stirling, but with the hard, flat-planed body of an athlete. His face was handsome except for the faint slackness of the muscles around the mouth, which often can be seen on a person who is mute. The ruddy light

53

from the fire glinted on the circular voice box attached to his throat.

Stirling smiled easily, aware that he was adopting the familiar big-brother attitude in a reflexive defence against a situation which alarmed him.

"Hello Johnny," he said, and moved his arms helplessly in their bindings. "Sorry I can't shake hands with you."

## Chapter Seven

"So it came at you, did it? Arms going like windmills?"

Johnny laughed with boyish pleasure, and the others in the hut joined in. Stirling was vaguely aware of imperfections in the sound of his brother's laugh – a kind of skidding clash of chords which suggested the voice box needed overhauling – but he was too busy eating to give it much thought. The soup tasted incredibly good, and not merely because he was hungry. It was made from at least six different vegetables, some of which Stirling had never seen before, and had been simmered slowly, perhaps for days, into a thick, nearly homogeneous slurry which he was unable to stop devouring. The FTA had worked wonders down below, he thought, but this is *food*.

Stirling smiled compliantly between mouthfuls. "That's right. Bright red, it was. Arms going like windmills. What was it?"

"I'm surprised at you, Vic. I thought you newspapermen had read everything and knew even more." Johnny was enjoying himself. "Farmers have always used scarecrows, haven't they?"

"A scarecrow! But . . ." A whole universe of angry darkness yawned momentarily beneath Stirling's feet. "But we're five kilometres above sea level. Birds don't fly that high, do they? Five kilometres?"

"Some of them do – geese, mainly. On a clear day you can see them going over here, so far up they look like specks of dust; and your insides feel empty with watching them. I'm told the Iles attract geese. In the old days they used to come around here in thousands and foul up the transit area; so, the scarecrows were put in. There're a few machines at this end of the raft too, but we keep them immobilised most of the time; otherwise we'd get nothing in the traps."

Stirling noted the frequent use of the personal plural. His brother's apparently complete identification with the group on the Ile could mean it would be difficult to persuade him to return; but that was something to worry about later. For the moment he was content just to rest, eat, and enjoy the curiously archaic pleasures of being with and talking to his own kin. The last was a very real enjoyment in spite of the fact that it must have been, in part, induced by the bizarre circumstances of the meeting. Down below, Stirling had left the fam-apt at the first opportunity and had never thought about Johnny from one year to the next. Up here on the Ile, drifting above cloud-mountains, the family connection was important; and it felt strong even though Johnny had changed.

And Johnny *was* different. Looking at him in the dim light of an almost-exhausted glow-globe strung in the roof, Stirling saw that his brother had lost the odd mixture of timidity and truculence which had made him virtually unemployable since his teens. He was relaxed, confident, exuding a kind of exultant pleasure in being alive. The only thing which appeared not to have changed was Johnny's pride in his physique. It was neither warm nor cold in the hut, and all the others were fully clad in assorted old clothes, but Johnny was stripped to the waist. The flat swathes of muscle across his shoulders and chest had an inhuman hardness, a crispness of definition which made them look like the body plates of an armoured creature.

Behind him stood Stirling's two captors, Dix and Paddy; and crouched around the hut in postures of uneasy watchfulness were four other men, none of whom had spoken a word. Stirling was reminded that his brother was known among them as "Jaycee" – a man who, from the stray references picked up during the long walk to the village, had come among them and immediately assumed command, apparently through sheer force. This was something Stirling found difficulty in assimilating. Johnny had always been bigger and stronger than most people; but the will to rule others was something new in his character.

"My brother will sleep here," Johnny said abruptly. "Tell Melissa to bring him some bedding from the store and make it up."

"Sure thing, Jaycee," Dix pushed himself away from the wall and headed for the door. He was a rangy, brown man with prematurely silver hair and protruding lower jaw.

"It's very late," Paddy said quietly. "She'll be asleep, and old Latham won't like anybody going into their place at this time of night." The glow-globe had revealed him as having a flattened nose and reproachful brown eyes, the face of a man who has seen everything and failed to benefit from the experience.

Dix lifted his shoulders in exasperation. "That old goat Latham! I hope he objects. I just hope he objects." He grinned, showing only his lower teeth. "I wouldn't mind if Melissa tried to throw me out, too."

Stirling felt his animosity for the man return. "This man Latham, Johnny. He's pretty old, is he?"

"Yeah. Melissa's father is pretty old."

"I thought so. I could see Dix was getting ready to bump him, so I guessed he must be an old man." This is childish, Stirling thought, but the techniques you learn for picking fights at school are always the best simply because they are childish. "Either that, or Dix is planning to sneak up and club him from the back the way he did with me tonight."

Dix, his eyes sick with hatred, stared at Stirling, but did not speak. Stirling guessed it must have been a bitter blow to him when his new capture had turned out to be Jaycee's brother.

Johnny looked concerned. "Did he hurt you, Vic?"

"I didn't hurt him, Jaycee," Dix protested. "He was able to walk in here, wasn't he? He was only out for a few seconds."

"That part could be true," Stirling said. "When I woke up he was still emptying my pockets."

Dix, his mouth working silently, took an involuntary half-step towards Stirling, but checked himself as Johnny stood up.

57

"I'll talk to you later, Dix." The slight distortions produced by the voice box made Johnny's words menacingly flat.

Dix spread his knobby-fingered hands. "How was I to know . . .?"

"Give my brother back what you took; then fetch Melissa. And don't make any more trouble."

"Sure thing, Jaycee." Dix lifted Stirling's pack from a corner, dropped it in his lap, and went out with a venomous glance over his shoulder. Stirling lifted the pack, set it by his side, and when he looked up found Johnny's eyes on him.

"How did you find me, Vic?"

"Mostly luck, I guess. I noticed you took Dad Considine's boots."

"Well, I'll be damned," Johnny said in wonderment. "You mean you can remember all that stuff we talked about when we were kids?"

"Sure. Why not?"

"I didn't think you would. You seemed to grow up so fast and get out so fast. I'm surprised you can remember it, that's all."

Stirling felt uncomfortable, guilty. "Listen, Johnny. I know I wasn't much of a brother just at the time when you needed me . . ."

"Who needed you?"

"I'll put that another way . . ."

"Save your breath, Victor. I'm all right, and I don't need an amateur analyst."

"I'm trying to get things straight between us."

Johnny smiled. "Vic, how many people did you know down there who had single apartments like your own?" He used an old trick Stirling had almost forgotten: speaking through the voice box while his lips remained motionless in the smile. In their private convention, this meant triumph, the conversational equivalent of "checkmate".

"What do you mean?" Stirling uneasily sifted the connotations of the question.

"Let's put it another way – how do you feel right now?"

"Pretty tired. *Very tired*."

"But otherwise all right?"

"I guess so. Why?"

"Some people spend their first week up here lying on their bellies, hugging the dirt, afraid to move. Some of them die. That skull you found was probably all that's left of somebody who got up the ladder and was too paralysed by agoraphobia to get out of the scarecrow's way. The sky leans heavily on some men, Vic."

Stirling inventoried his own emotions. Johnny was wrong about him. He *could* feel those kilometres of thin, cold air underneath, and his nerves shrieked out against them. Yet he had walked a long way across Heaven on his first day. And there had been a skull buried in the soil only a few paces from the transit area.

There was a sound at the entrance to the hut, and a young woman came in carrying an armful of lumpy pillows covered in plastic. Moving so quickly that Stirling had barely time to focus on her in the dim light, she threw the pillows onto the floor and stalked out. He got an impression of a black whiplash of a woman: lean, hard, impossibly thick hair exploding darkly away from her temples, eyes signalling anger. One of the men sitting near the door grabbed for her playfully as she went by; there was the sound of a slap; he settled back against the wall and ruefully nursed his cheek while the others laughed uproariously. Stirling blinked. He had not even seen the blow.

"That was Melissa." Johnny spoke with a kind of proprietary pride. "What do you think of her, Vic?"

"Nice," Stirling said cautiously.

"Nice, he says. That's the future Mrs Considine."

"Does she know it yet?"

Johnny laughed. "That's the sort of crack you were always best at, Vic. The big, soft man who carries a stiletto! Melissa knows about it, all right – she just enjoys acting mad like that. It's a kind of ritual with women like her. A prenuptial ritual."

"What's she doing up here anyway?"

"She *lives* here."

"How did she get here?"

"That's a long story." Johnny glanced around benignly at the other men squatting against the walls; he did it strangely, like a savage king surveying his court. "Her father brought her up about fifteen years ago when she was just a kid. You'll never guess what old Latham was before he came here."

"Tell me," Stirling said. *Fifteen years*, he thought, *fifteen years of this*.

"A judge," Johnny announced. "Imagine a high court judge breaking out of the Compression! It's fair enough, I suppose, but he set himself up as a judge up here too. A real little philosopher-king, he was.

"When I arrived he watched me for a couple of days out of those watery old eyes and told me he had assessed me. *Assessed* me! He said I was best suited for foraging. I was to cover a whole 24-kilometre strip by myself, breaking off an ear of corn or something every hundred paces so as not to cause a localised drop in the harvest – which would be noticed down in the station." Johnny snorted – one of the few sounds he could make naturally, without the aid of the vocal prosthetic.

"You didn't like the idea," Stirling said.

"You bet I didn't. People were always assessing me down below and coming out with the wrong answers. I told him I was going to sit in the village all day, and he was going to forage. I told him I was going to do all the assessing from now on." Johnny savoured the memory for a few seconds before he went on.

"Old man Latham kicked up hell. He called in his own little law-enforcement agency, a big dumb hulk called . . ."

"Luciano," one of the listeners supplied.

"That's it. Luciano. The only thing was, I did all the enforcing." Johnny glanced down complacently at his broad, flat forearms.

"You didn't kill him?"

"Of course not. He's foraging too now. Along with Judge Latham. I saw him a couple of days ago and" – Johnny winked broadly at the other men – "he's walking almost normally again."

There was a ripple of amusement which took in everybody except, Stirling noticed, the man called Paddy. He stared at his brother in disbelief. Two short months in the Stone-Age society of the Ile had turned Johnny Considine into a stranger. Could this really be the kid brother he had protected all the way through junior school because his classmates had ribbed him so much about the voice box? Stirling's eyes instinctively searched for and found the L-shaped scar on Johnny's throat. It had been shortly after Johnny's fourth birthday when he had fallen, while carrying a drinking glass, and a transparent spear had gouged its way through his vocal cords. He was wrong, Stirling realised, to think that Johnny had changed, but the new environment was developing latent aspects of his character which would be better kept in the background. This is my big-brother act again, Stirling thought, but family responsibilities must mean something. He remembered, with a stirring of guilt, that neither of them had yet mentioned their mother. Filled with a sudden sense of urgency, Stirling tried for something significant to say, but then became aware of the incongruity of the two of them sorting out their family problems before an audience of strangers.

"Johnny," he said, "I've got things I want to discuss with you, in private."

"This is private."

"This is the Ile's equivalent of Grand Central station."

"Things are different up here. I don't have any secrets from the other members of the Council."

"Get rid of them, Johnny."

Johnny's eyes clouded with something like pain. "There are things you'll have to learn, Vic, and I think it's going to be hard on both of us. Come on – I'll show you around."

He got up and left the hut with a dismissive wave to the rest of the group. As Stirling followed him out, he had to stoop to pass through the doorway with its curtain of the same black plastic used on the Ile for clothing. The night breezes were cool, but not nearly as cold as Stirling had expected at the altitude.

"Greenhouse effect," Johnny explained as they walked. "There's a shell field covering the whole productive area of the Ile. The intensity's very low – a goose can fly right through it without even blinking – but it's enough to increase the wavelength of solar radiations coming through, and the heat doesn't get back out again. Keeps in most of the oxygen all this green stuff gives off, which is a good thing for us too."

"So you didn't need the big boots, after all."

"No. I didn't need the big boots."

Stirling took a deep breath. "Johnny, this whole business is a charade. You can't go on hiding up here, chief of a tribe of dropouts."

"Why not?"

"Because it's too fantastic. Normal people don't live like this. And think of your mother."

"Oh, brother! Are you scraping the bottom of the barrel!"

"All right," Stirling said. "That sounded corny, even to me. But what about her?"

"Mother knows I can look after myself and that I'm not the suicidal type. You know, Vic, that's good, coming from you. You got out just as soon as you were able, and you never took time off to visit her even though you were only a few blocks away."

"I'm not proud of that, but mother doesn't really need people much."

"Precisely my point, big brother. So why bring her into it? This is purely between us. How about getting down to the real reason you came after me?"

"Which is . . . ?"

"Which is that you hated it down there as much as I did. You got your newspaper job and poured your salary into a single apartment because that was the only escape you could visualise. And when I got right out of the whole setup, *really* escaped from the whole stinking mess down there, it made you sick.

62

"You want to bring me back because you couldn't have gone on living in the Compression knowing I was up here. It's the post-1996 situation all over again on a smaller scale. When the Government set out to brainwash everybody into thinking they liked living like sardines, they ruled that nobody would be allowed to live on the Iles because the Compression could only be made bearable if *everybody* was in it together. No favourites. No bending the law for the rich and the powerful, wasn't that it, big brother? That's why you came after me. Admit it."

Stirling could feel depths which dwarfed the five-kilometre fall from Heaven opening up under his feet. "You couldn't be further off the beam, Johnny. You're my brother . . ."

"Half-brother," Johnny interrupted in a voice which sounded like an electrical discharge in the prosthetic. He turned to face Stirling. "My father was not your father."

"It makes no difference to me."

"Victor! While we're at it, let's dig down even deeper. Let's say the one thing which has never been said before."

Stirling suddenly felt tired, defeated. "Let's get some sleep and talk this over in the morning."

"You and I," Johnny said slowly and distinctly. "We never liked each other."

Stirling was conscious of no pain, no torment, only a feeling of release as deep-seated tensions ebbed away. The psychic discharge brought him a few moments of cool, blessed sanity. He stared past Johnny towards the night-black fields and the ancient gleams of the cooking fires. He saw them with new eyes. This was . . . freedom.

"My kid brother has grown up and passed me," he said finally. "I'll leave in the morning."

"I'm sorry," Johnny replied softly. "Nobody goes back down."

"What?"

"It's the only real law we have in Heaven. Do you think nobody ever tried the life, then changed his mind? This community depends on secrecy; and the only way we can be sure of getting it, is by never allowing anyone to go back.

"From now on, big brother, you're permanently on the side of the angels."

# Chapter Eight

The village occupied the southeast corner of the Ile, and housed some two hundred people. Women made up about a fourth of the population; but, although the majority of them had paired off with men, Stirling had seen no children during his brief survey. He guessed that even rebel women would be too practical to take off into the blue without packing a lifelong supply of oral contraceptives. At a rate of one pill a month, a small handful would be enough to secure permanently the doors of life. Yet, the rigid control of the birth rate was one of the most irksome features of life in the Compression – Stirling thought briefly of the anonymous couple whose bodies in the river had indirectly triggered the events which brought him to Heaven – and he would have expected those restraints to be the first to go. He made up his mind to ask someone about it before he left the Ile for good.

His fourth morning on the raft was exactly like the previous three: an affair of achingly pure blue sky, pastel mists, the sober green geometries of the soil beds, sunlight splintering through transient treasures of dew. Stirling filled his lungs with it gratefully as he crawled out of his personal burrow and began to prepare for the day's work.

The people of the Ile built no real houses, partly through lack of structural materials, partly because of the risk of attracting the attention of transatlantic jet crews. Because its air was comparatively warm and moist, a milky canopy of water vapour was usually drawn across the underside of the Ile's shell field; but there was always the chance that some sharp-eyed pilot would penetrate the screen. Transatlantic air travel had never regained the peak it had achieved before the

War, before the country had curled up on itself like a wounded animal; but International Land Extension, US 23, was close to the main trade arteries. The daily freighter, carrying the token food gifts from India, seemed to take a particular pleasure in coming in low over the raft and freezing the people of the village in their tracks. Stirling had considered signalling to one of the planes; but he would have been more likely to attract the attention of the people around him; and this was the last thing his plans required.

It had taken every shred of his self-control not to run in blind panic when Johnny told him there was no going back. He had shrugged, admitted the validity of Johnny's analysis of his motives, and asked for a job. The gamble had been that a man, who was sufficiently unbalanced to choose to live on the Ile, would accept the story.

"Hi there, Vic. Ready for the day's work?"

Stirling nodded and smiled as Pete Biquard approached. Every man on the Ile was lean and brown, Stirling had noticed; but Biquard was stringier than most, and his skin was almost chestnut in colour. His tattered but functional clothing, slitted eyes and loose, easy walk made him look like a re-creation of the classical frontiersman. Stirling was sure Biquard had been specially appointed to work with him because of his loyalty to Johnny and the Council, but he found himself liking the other man.

"How far are we going today, Pete?"

Biquard screwed up his face in thought. "We oughtta go right up to the northeast corner – I ain't been up that way in nearly a week. Do you think you could drag that overweight carcass of yours that far?"

"I could do it with your skinny carcass on my back," Stirling replied in mock belligerence. "How long will it take us?"

"Depends on how much stuff we get. Allow two hours to reach the corner, mebbe three coming back. If we get a haul of structural plastic, it could take even longer."

"What sort of plastic?"

66

"We call it structural because it's good for building huts and roofing burrows. Actually it's covers from the shellfield booster units around the perimeter. They're on the outside of the wall. So you can't see them from here. Some of them get crisped up a bit by lightning strikes, and the maintenance robots dump them in a salvage depot in the northeast corner."

"Aren't the quantities that go back for salvage checked?"

"We don't take complete covers – just some ribs and odd pieces of skin. You're nearly as nosy as that brother of yours was when he first got here." Biquard studied Stirling's face with inquisitive blue eyes.

"Let's get something to eat," Stirling said.

A sheltered area under a raised water tank housed the communal soup kitchen at which the foraging and scavenging teams ate before setting out. As they walked towards it, Stirling calculated his chances of a successful break. He and Biquard were going out on a five-hour trip. If they travelled north for an hour, they should be just about on the Ile's longitudinal axis, at which point – if Stirling broke free – he would have a straight 24-kilometre slog to the transit area. With the sort of start he would have, his chances of reaching the elevator were excellent. It was difficult to imagine even Johnny's tireless, weatherbeaten lieutenants catching him if he got so much as a single hour's lead.

The smell of the now familiar soup distracted Stirling as he and Biquard reached the water tower. A dozen men were standing or squatting around, eating from crudely formed plastic plates. They greeted Biquard enthusiastically; most of them included Stirling in their welcome, but with varying degrees of reserve. He had no way of telling how much his reception had been influenced, one way or the other, by his relationship to Johnny. None of the men ever discussed "Jaycee" in Stirling's presence, and he had not seen his brother, except at a distance, since the night he arrived. Each time Johnny had waved with ironic courtesy and gone his way, accompanied by Dix and other Council members. It seemed that the break between the brothers had been as clean as it was sudden. Johnny apparently spent most of his time in discussions – unimaginable to Stirling – which he treated with all the seriousness of a statesman controlling the destinies of billions. There were moments when Stirling found it difficult to realise that this fantastic holiday from reality was taking place within sight of the East Coast conurbation. Did all the other Iles scattered around the coast have their own little colonies? Their own petty dictators parading minute armies across microscopic dominions?

Stirling went under the tower with Biquard and was served a generous helping of the thick, aromatic soup by a middle-aged woman dressed in the usual makeshifts of black plastic and faded textiles. As he stood, scooping the hot food into his mouth, he caught sight of Melissa Latham moving through the shade beyond the line of cooking fires. Her mass of jet-black hair was loosely brushed back, and her slim body was snake-like in its glistening wrappings of black plastic. She glanced in his direction, and he instinctively raised his hand in a half-salute. Instantly, she turned away, and he felt an odd flicker of pleasure at having been recognised. Watch it, Stirling, he thought. This is no time to try the "What's-a-nice-kid-like-you-doing-in-a-joint-like-this?" routine.

"You can't have her, Vic." Biquard spoke into Stirling's ear from close up and startled him.

"I understand Jaycee has spoken for her."

"He has. But that ain't the reason. Her old man ain't letting her pair off with anybody."

"Not even with Jaycee?" Stirling probed gently, surprised at the extent of his own interest.

"Not even with Jaycee. Judge Latham's daughter is a cut above any of the men around these parts." Biquard snorted into his soup. "Still, there's no need for you to worry none, Vic. Not all the women are so stand-offish. A handsome, big guy like you won't have no trouble. I'll introduce you to a couple of real friendly girls tonight – you should have mentioned it sooner."

"I haven't mentioned anything yet," Stirling pointed out drily, then brought the conversation back to the point which interested him most.

"If Melissa has such a high opinion of herself, why does she let Johnny order her around so much?"

Biquard looked knowing. "The judge is a sick man. Melissa's scared to kick up too much fuss in case Jaycee turns real nasty and frightens the old man to death. And mebbe she don't want to put Jaycee right off her. When the judge goes, there's going to be a big rush for that dame. She'd be better off with Jaycee than with some of the cave men we have around here, even if he does play it a bit rough at times."

When they had finished eating, Stirling and Biquard began walking north along the margin, but skirted the fertiliser pits and raised tanks of water and agricultural chemicals. Twice they had to get out of the way as the big robots trundled clear of the soil beds to let their arms and hoses scoop up supplies. A complex of metal tracks ran the length of the margin at right angles to the main rails. This enabled the robots to be diverted to other strips. Here and there stood bright red scarecrows, all identical to the one which had gone for Stirling on his arrival in the transit area. With their heat-sensitive receptors deactivated, the lurid machines stood quietly in the morning sunlight, their multiple arms hanging at their sides. It occurred to Stirling that some of the rebels must have a fair amount of electronic knowledge.

On the way north, finding Biquard still in the mood to talk, he returned to the subject of Melissa Latham and Johnny. As near as he could determine it from the other man's deliberately oblique answers, the situation on the Ile was that most of the villagers had acquiesced in Johnny's abrupt take-over. It made little difference to them whether their infrequent orders came from Judge Latham or Jaycee, as long as they had enough time between jobs to sit about and drink their homemade liquor. But there was a sizable group which had objected to Jaycee and the men he had chosen as his Council. Stirling got the impression that, while Johnny had become an enthusiastic proponent of power politics in his microcosm, he would find "marriage" to Melissa a valuable asset.

For perhaps the thousandth time since his arrival on the Ile, he marvelled at its self-contained, clinical demonstration of man's inability to live in any sort of a community without someone claiming the right to be in command. Or, perhaps, Johnny had no positive desire to give orders, just the need to escape receiving them. If Judge Latham had not "assessed" him, things might have turned out differently. As Johnny had said, other people had been assessing him all his life and coming up with the wrong answers. Stirling made up his mind on the spur of the moment that, when he got back down on the ground, he would keep quiet about the rebel colony. He could claim he had taken the trip as a stunt, which would make some excellent news copy. And it would, too, if the FTA ever let it get into print.

As they walked, Stirling took every opportunity to step up onto tank support structures and look along the varicoloured strips tapering away into the distance, like threads gathered into perspective's fist. Gradually, the shimmering, white oblong of the Ile's central power station moved across his field of vision until he judged he was right on the longitudinal axis.

Biquard had set a cracking eight kilometres an hour for the walk and had grown used to his companion constantly lagging behind. Stirling unhitched the coil of high-tensile plastic which had been provided for lashing anything the scavenging expedition produced. He closed the gap between himself and Biquard, and got ready to loop the coil over Biquard's head and shoulders, then regretfully decided it could be too risky. The rangy oldster moved as though he was powered by steel springs; and, if he got the chance to run, Stirling would never catch him. There was too much at stake.

Stirling got in close, chopped downwards behind Biquard's ear, and sent him down on one knee. He threw the rope around Biquard's arms and a second later found himself struggling with a sinewy ball of fury – like a trout angler who had hooked a shark.

70

"I'm sorry, Pete," Stirling grunted. "I was trying to avoid this." He punched Biquard under the ribs, this time putting his full weight into it. A full two minutes went by before Biquard's eyes began to open, and by then Stirling had trussed him securely. He dragged the older man into the shadow of a tank and made him as comfortable as possible under the circumstances.

"You're a fool," Biquard wheezed. "Nobody has ever made it. And you won't."

"Only one way to find out, Pete. I'm sorry about hitting you. Tell Jaycee I'm not going to give away any secrets down below."

"You bet you ain't. There's a . . ."

Stirling ran across the lateral tracks and plunged into a green alley of bean plants, which immediately shut out most of the mid-morning light. He kept up his speed for several hundred metres, then realised he was likely to sprain an ankle on the closely spaced rails. Giving in to the fact that he was not built for long-distance running anyway, he slowed down to a fast walk, occasionally stumbling as he misjudged the interval between the sleepers.

At first a fierce sense of urgency drove him on, but the minutes stretched out in safety. By the time he had been travelling through the green blankets of summer silence for half an hour, he began to relax a little. After another thirty minutes he climbed up to soil bed level and took his bearings. The power station marking the Ile's central point was about two kilometres ahead and slightly to his right. Behind him, Heaven's broad acres slumbered in utter peace. Even the random, yellow flecks of the robots seemed to be at rest.

Stirling kept his elation in check until he had passed the featureless block of the power station; then he began to grin furiously as he struggled to maintain speed. He did not know how many villagers would be travelling the eastern margin; but even if they had found Biquard almost right away, it would have taken them some time to organise a pursuit party. A group would be necessary because – Stirling felt adrenalin boost his muscle power – having got this far, he was not going to be stopped by one, two or three men.

He became aware of the rail beneath his left foot thrumming slightly; it meant a robot was approaching from the direction of the transit area. Stirling kept a wary eye ahead and saw the massive yellow structure in good time. Feeling pleased with his newly acquired expertise in the ways of Heaven, he climbed into the soil bed on his right and nestled down into the cool green stalks. The robot swept by, its turret hanging impassively from the thirty-metre beam, and disappeared to the east, moving at a ponderous eighty kilometres an hour. He remembered with a feather-flick of unease that the only other time he had seen a robot do its maximum speed was on his first eventful day, but he was unable to pin down any reason why some part of his mind should feel alarm over the fact. The halfway mark was well behind him now, and he was moving as fast as when he had set out.

Ten minutes later he passed the robot tending the strip to his right. The spider legs moved listlessly below its turret and hissed chemicals into their submissive charges while the servos hummed faintly in the downy air. By the time the robot had dwindled out of sight in the leafy vee behind him, Stirling was beginning to tire. He had covered upwards of more than twenty kilometres since leaving the village – most of them under difficult walking conditions, and his thighs were protesting at each step. But this was the last lap, and the structures of the transit area would soon be looming up in front. Once he got in view of the monitor cameras, Johnny and the others would have to let him go down and take their chance on his keeping silent. He began to think about the Ile in past tense. *Heaven!* Stirling found it almost impossible to make his mind bridge the gap between the fairy tale vision of his childhood and the hard, practical reality. Think of it this way. *You're not gaining a father, but losing a brother.* Yet, the excursion had paid off in some respects. The discovery that he was not his brother's keeper had been an important one. All his life he had been climbing a long, steep hill; then someone had told him there was no need, that he should turn back; now he was running downhill, travelling fast and free.

The rail under his left foot began to vibrate. Stirling frowned as he tried to quicken his pace. The robot which had passed him was coming back, still moving at top speed. There was no denying that this was an unusual amount of activity for one of the big machines; but, perhaps, his presence was upsetting some receptor network. He kept glancing back over his shoulder until the familiar yellow angularities appeared, flaring in the brilliant light; then he rolled into the soil bed on his right and lay still. A green, private universe. It would be so pleasant to rest here among the cool stalks and sleep. The vibrations coming up through the soil reached their climax, and his green cave darkened momentarily as the robot's superstructure blotted out the light.

"There he is!" The voice seemed to come from the sky.

Stirling barely had time to glimpse the black, tattered, flying silhouettes against the sky's blue canopy. Something hard and heavy smashed down on him with irresistible force. His face was driven down into the dark soil, in which he had once found a human skull.

## Chapter Nine

"Next time, of course, we'll have to kill you."

Johnny Considine paced the floor of the stockade as he spoke. In the reddish evening light his sharply defined muscles, with their clearly visible insertions, reminded Stirling more than ever of a crab's body plates. The voice box shone at his throat like a medallion.

"You mean, you're giving me a chance. I'm grateful." Stirling tried to sound calm and relaxed, but his mind was seething with disappointment and shock. The villagers had ridden the great robot, controlling it like a horse or camel. *How?*

"I didn't ask you to come here, Victor. Don't forget that. You're alive at this minute only because of your relationship to me."

Stirling laughed bitterly. "I notice that all your loyal subjects call you 'Jaycee', Johnny. Do I detect a religious connotation there? After all, this *is* Heaven."

"You must have thought I was pretty stupid," Johnny said impassively. "Didn't you think it was odd for a new member, still on probation, to be put on scavenging patrol?"

"We are always in the forge, or on the anvil," Stirling quoted. "By trials God is shaping us for . . ."

"Cut that stuff!"

"All right, Johnny. I guess I didn't give you enough credit for brains, but can't you give me credit for not being malicious? I left word with Pete Biquard that I would never talk about what I've seen here, and I meant it. I don't want to pull your little world out from under your feet."

"It's no use, Victor. You don't seem to understand that

74

you've come among people who can't even *breathe* down below. I mean it. There were nights when my heart felt like a pillow filling my whole chest. I used to lie inside that box and do nothing but try to get air inside me, and I never got enough.

"Most of the villagers were worse than I was. To them, going back down would be the exact equivalent of dying: that's why they'll never let you go. It's two hundred lives against your one, Victor."

"But you're the boss man here," Stirling said reasonably. "Surely . . ."

"It's my life, too." Johnny's voice was a discordant shriek from the prosthetic. "From now on, you and I are not brothers, Victor. Look out for yourself."

Johnny went out, and someone lashed the door shut from the outside. Stirling stared after him for a moment, then walked around his new home. The stockade was a ten-metre-square space under one of the smaller storage tanks. Its metal underside formed a two-metre-high ceiling, and the walls were of scavenged plastic wired to the tank's stanchions and diagonal bracing. Not an escape-proof prison by any means; but a constant watch would be kept; and, if he did get out, there would be the same 24-kilometre slog to the transit area. With ragged warriors hounding him down, from the backs of their metal dinosaurs.

In a corner of the stockade someone had left Stirling's foam-insulated sleeping bag in an untidy bundle. He zipped himself into it and lay staring at the streaked metal plates over his head.

*First*, he thought, *first catch your dinosaur . . .*

He wakened in the morning to the sound of the door being opened. Stirling sat up, rubbed his eyes, and saw Melissa Latham come in carrying a tray. Strips of sunlight from the cracks in the walls snaked across her body as she stooped to set the tray on the floor.

"Thank you. I'm ready for that – I guess I didn't get much to eat yesterday." Stirling kept his voice polite and neutral, waiting for clues which would let him assess the situation. Here

75

was one person who would know even more than Johnny about the villagers, including the technique of controlling the big robots. She would have to be courted with all the delicacy and insight of which he was capable, and he hoped he could muster more of both qualities than he had shown in his dealings with Johnny.

Melissa nodded watchfully, without speaking, and made no move to leave. Stirling tried to unzip his sleeping bag; but avenues of pain opened up right across his back. His ribs and shoulders had stiffened into near-immobility during the night – somebody had worked him over, hard, after his capture. He thought he could guess who.

"I don't know what status enemies of the state have up here, Miss Latham," he said as he made a second and more cautious attempt to open the bag, "but may I ask you one question?"

"What is it?"

"Was that slightly simian gentleman known as Dix one of the party who brought me back here yesterday?"

"Don't you remember?"

"No. I was . . . dozing at the time."

"Yes, Dix was there. Why do you ask?"

"I'm a very conscientious person," Stirling said, deciding he could use Dix as a means of testing Melissa's attitude to several aspects of life on the Ile. "When somebody gives me something, I like to make sure he gets it back – and Dix is building up quite an account for himself."

Melissa almost smiled. Reaction satisfactory, Stirling thought, but why is she hanging around here, listening to me? Any animal magnetism I might have had wouldn't have survived the degaussing of the last few days. He finished struggling out of the bag, lifted the tray, and began to eat.

"Are you really his brother?"

"Half-brother." Stirling looked up at Melissa. So that was it. She was interested in him because of his connection with Johnny. He felt an irrational flicker of disappointment.

"He never mentioned you."

76

"I didn't talk much about him either. It's all slightly pathetic. Are you really his girl friend?" Too far and too fast, he thought immediately; but she shrugged casually and leaned against the wall. Stirling got his first good look at her face and approved of what he saw. Flawless, brown skin stretched in economical planes, dark eyes with almost phosphorescent whites, lips which would be sensitive or sensual depending on how a man looked at her, or how she looked at him.

"My father wants to see you," she said.

"Why?"

"He sees every new member."

"Oh, yes. The traditional interview with the village elder. I thought Johnny had done away with all that."

"He would like to, but a lot of people remember my father lifted this village out of the Stone Age when he came here. He won't be cast aside so easily, no matter what you or your brother think."

"Hold on a minute! *I* don't want to cast him aside. All I want is to get off the Ile – that's why I'm in here, remember."

"That's an even more futile ambition than your brother's. Nobody goes back."

Stirling nodded disbelievingly. "When do I see your father?"

"He would like you to come along to our hut during your lunch break today."

"You mean I'm allowed to go outside?"

"Of course. If prisoners did no work, we'd have a queue waiting to get into the stockade. No work, no food."

"Is that the *lex non scripta*?"

"My father will write the law out for you, if necessary," Melissa said curtly, demonstrating that she had understood the Latin tag. As if to further emphasise the point, she lifted the tray from Stirling's lap before he had quite finished, and went out with it. Her massive battle-plume of black hair was momentarily limned with bronze by the morning light, then the door closed behind her. Stirling got up and folded away his sleeping bag, uneasily aware that Melissa's after-image was persisting an unusually long time.

77

He spent the morning emptying bird traps from plastic sacks, checking and repairing the mechanisms, and coating them with goose grease. The traps were treacherous devices made from metal scraps over a period of many years by men with different ideas and varying standards of professionalism. In the comparatively moist, oxygen-rich atmosphere of the Ile, the rate of oxidisation of unprotected ferrous metals was high and added to the unreliability of the traps. Stirling found it necessary to give the work all his attention in the interests of retaining a complete set of fingers; and the time passed quickly.

A constant stream of villagers, thin, brown individuals who showed an amiable curiosity about Stirling's personal background, came by the storage hut beside which he was working. Although there was no marriage or giving in marriage in Heaven, a good proportion of them were paired off in apparent monogamy, and he saw – at last – several children. They seemed to have no ambition in life but to eat, sleep, and gather food. The sinless, blameless life of a primitive tribe seemed to suit them perfectly: they were super-hoboes riding a celestial freight car on a journey to nowhere. Stirling tried without success to see things from their point of view. The Compression was bad – but not all that bad.

Late in the morning Pete Biquard came by, carrying a load of the thin black plastic used so much by the villagers. This plastic, Stirling had learned, was the standard weather-proofing for robot replacement units. He spoke briefly, completely without animosity; but Stirling got the impression Biquard realised he had been chosen as the guinea pig for Johnny's trial of his brother's trustworthiness, and was not happy about it. Stirling filed the fact away for possible future use.

At lunchtime the middle-aged woman who had served him the previous morning brought a tray of food, much of it uncooked lettuce and cabbage dressed with green-flecked vegetable oil. Stirling suspected his new diet was deficient in protein; but he was feeling better than ever before in his life and already had detected a certain roominess in the waistband of his trousers. The grey uniform supplied by Bennett less than a week earlier was dirty, torn, and stained with blood and goose fat, but Stirling preferred it to the black plastic. He cleaned up his tray and tentatively began walking in the direction in which he believed the Lathams' hut to lie.

Apart from the man whom he vaguely remembered – from his first night – as a Council member and who had directed him to his work on the traps, Stirling had seen no evidence that he was under guard. His leaving the vicinity of the storage hut would give an indication of how much prison life on the Ile differed from its counterpart kilometres below. Stirling had once visited Newburyport's main penitentiary, but had locked the memory away in a place where it would not easily be stumbled upon.

Immediately after he began to walk, a small, blackened stick of a man, who had been sleeping against a storage bin, got to his feet and moved after him. Stirling gave the little man a contented wave – this amount of surveillance he could stand – and concentrated on finding the Lathams' hut. The villagers had made a good job of protecting their dwellings from inquisitive eyes or satellite-borne cameras. The surface of the Ile outside the area occupied by the soil beds was covered by a brown lightweight composition; but it had been silted over with the dust of many summers, and insouciant grasses had taken hold. In the kilometre length of the village most of the elevated tank structures had been adapted as living quarters, and the individual foxholes constructed in the open were roofed with matted straw and leaves. Even at close range, a casual observer glancing along the eastern margin was likely to see nothing but complex rail systems and an occasional agricultural robot satisfying its appetites at the grass-blurred tanks.

Stirling found the Latham place in about ten minutes, with some assistance from passers-by. It was constructed on the same lines as the stockade and was considerably larger than most of the villagers' private dwellings. He knocked at the low

79

entrance and a thin but hoarse voice told him to enter. Inside he found the hut was divided into several rooms by woven grass screens. In the room to his right he found an old man lying on a low bed which was covered in genuine fabrics. The man raised himself on one arm.

"Are you Victor Stirling?"

"That's right."

"What's right? I didn't make any statement – I only asked you a question, so how could anything be 'right'?" Judge Latham's blurry, grey eyes fixed themselves ferociously on Stirling's face for a few seconds; then he gave a triumphant smile. "You journalists! Biggest butchers of the language I've ever seen. You get your money for nothing. You know that, don't you?"

"My editor often said that too, Judge," Stirling replied, grinning. "I never appreciated his viewpoint."

"You probably gave him ulcers. Well, don't stand there blocking the light. Pull up a heap of dust and sit down."

Stirling found a stool and tested his weight on it carefully. Judge Latham sounded like a man he was going to like. He looked around the interior of the hut. He noted colour sketches on the walls and a grey box which looked as though it could contain a micro-library.

"Melissa isn't here," Latham said abruptly. "Jaycee sent for her."

Stirling felt a pang of regret, then saw the older man was staring at him appraisingly. The pupils of the judge's eyes seemed almost to have dissolved into the whites; but his gaze went deep, and Stirling shifted uneasily. It was too soon for anyone to start thinking what the judge seemed to be thinking.

"She said you wanted to see me, Judge."

"Never mind the title, Victor. Call me Ford. My real name is Clifford, but it doesn't sound like a real name. Well, what do you think of my little place?" Latham stared at him eagerly from behind a nose which acne had turned into an enormous strawberry.

"It's the first *home* I've seen on the Ile," Stirling said.

Latham relaxed slightly. "What brought you up here, son?"

"I thought I was doing something for my brother. Now . . . What are you doing here?"

"Dying, mostly. Under the fourth sign of the zodiac."

"Cancer?" Stirling found the word difficult to say in the circumstances, but Latham seemed to have a detached interest in his own condition.

"You know your astrology, boy. It started over ten years ago; so I suppose I've been more fortunate than most."

"That's when you came up here?"

"That's when I came up here. It cost me a fortune in bribes."

"And you brought Melissa."

"She wanted to come. At the time I thought it would be only for a matter of months – a vacation in the sky – but things turned out differently. We both were lucky."

"Melissa too?"

"I said both of us were lucky." Latham leaned forward in the bed, and pain dragged his mouth out of shape. "My daughter is a *real* person. Did you meet any others down there?"

Stirling shook his head slowly and waited until the judge's breathing became easier. "I ask too many questions – it's an occupational disease."

"That's all right, son. This isn't one of my official interviews. I'm too old and sick now to play any real part in the village life; but I keep up the pretence just to annoy that so-called Council."

"That's a good enough reason, Ford." Stirling hesitated, judging his ground. "You know, it would really annoy them if I got away from here."

Latham let the words hang in the air for a few seconds before he shook his head. "You can put that idea right out of your head. This is a squalid, pointless little community in many ways, but I wouldn't betray it. Nobody goes back."

"Those words are beginning to stick in my throat," Stirling said tiredly. Then his interest revived. "You knew what I was going to ask you?"

Latham pushed his nose around delicately, as though moulding putty, and his eyes narrowed significantly. "I had an idea you might be developing an interest in the automatic cultivators."

"Well, they are fascinating machines."

"Have they any feature which particularly catches your interest?"

Stirling rubbed the heavy stubble on his chin, aware he was about to gamble. "I'm puzzled by the fact that machines designed for fully automatic operation on the Iles seem to have some kind of override circuit, making it possible for a human operator to give them arbitrary directions. Even from a distance."

"Now there's a thought." Latham toyed with the watch strapped to his narrow wrist. "If that were the case, you'd have five hundred getaway cars standing out there. All in a row. Believe me, son, there are no provisions on the robots for manual overriding; and if there were, I wouldn't tell you. Nobody . . ."

". . . goes back," Stirling completed the phrase and stood up. "Talking about going back, I think I should get to work. Have to make a good impression on the first day, you know."

Latham nodded wearily, but he held up one hand. "I like you, Victor. Possibly it's an indictment of our community that the only new member I have liked in ten years is the one who got here by mistake, but that's by the way . . .

"This is the only talk we'll ever have; yet there are so many things I'm not free to say. Melissa can't make her mind up about your brother. I have tried to help her come to a decision, but there are too many contradictions on both sides. It will take time . . . and that's something I'm running out of . . . You must forgive my incoherency, but the circumstances . . . I would put Melissa before Heaven itself . . ."

"You must rest, Judge."

"My name is Ford."

"Yes but 'Judge' suits you better. You've got to rest."

"How right . . . you are."

82

"I'll come and see you tomorrow, Judge." Stirling was uneasily aware that the old man had been trying to say something without putting it into words.

"No!" Latham's voice became stronger. "I'm receiving no more visitors. You journalists . . . money for nothing. Victor, take that thing with you. I've finished reading." Latham pointed to the grey box in the corner, then turned his face to the wall.

"Yes, sir." Stirling lifted the box and carried it out into the sunlight. It was a micro-library and, judging by its weight, a well-stocked one. He began walking back to the storage hut where the bird traps were kept, and at once the stick-like man stepped out of the shade to follow him.

The idea came so suddenly that it almost jolted Stirling into looking at the library's index panel in full view of his shadow. He waited, instead, until he was back at the heaps of traps and was squatting in the dust – ostensibly giving his full attention to the archaic mechanisms. While leaning over to scoop another handful of the evil-smelling goose grease, Stirling ran his eye down the printed plastic strips of the index.

One of them bore the words, *American Encyclopedia*. Stirling nodded in satisfaction. Had he been carrying out a routine research job back in the *Record*'s office, that was the book he would have chosen to give him information about the International Land Extensions and the design of their robots.

With his concentration on the traps broken, the hot hours of the afternoon dragged by like geological ages; and he received several rust-stained grazes on his fingers before someone came to let him know he had earned his food for the day. It was the man he knew as Paddy.

"You've been to the judge's place," he said, as Stirling stood up.

"Yes. Is it out of bounds?"

"Nope. Not out of bounds, but Jaycee won't like it much."

"Does it matter?" Stirling recalled his original walk to the village and how Paddy had been objecting to Johnny's new regime.

Paddy shrugged. "What have you got there?"

"The judge gave me his library. I presume I'll be permitted to read?"

"I used to be quite a reader myself," Paddy said reflectively. "Read a lot in the old days."

"I'm glad to hear it. It's always a pleasure to meet a fellow booklover."

Paddy gripped Stirling's arm, sinking his lean fingers into the muscle. "Keep the library, Stirling," he whispered, "but don't look down your nose at me. You and that brother of yours – you're great ones for using people."

Stirling watched the black figure stalking away through the village, somehow managing to look dignified in its flapping plastic wrappings; and then he realised he had been guilty of forgetting that the villagers were still members of the human race. He called out his thanks and took the micro-library into the stockade. The model was an unfamiliar one; and it took him several minutes to fit the reading glasses, connect up the flexible light-guides, and master the volume selection system. When he had the instrument working properly, he called up the encyclopedia. Perfect images of its microfilmed pages were carried through the corded light-guides from the enclosed projection system. Stirling adjusted the focus and worked through the index until he had the access coordinates for an article entitled: *International Land Extensions, automatic cultivation, engineering considerations.*

He punched in the article's coordinates and waited for the designated pages to appear. Instead of the expected closely printed page of text, an oblong of white brilliance sprang into view. In the centre of the field of light – looking crude and misshapen because of the magnifications concerned – somebody had printed three letters by hand. They were: "N.G.B."

After a moment's thought, Stirling decided they could stand for only one phrase.

*Nobody goes back.*

## Chapter Ten

"Where is Heaven? I cannot tell. Even to the eye of faith, Heaven looks much like a star to the eye of flesh. Set there on the brow of night, it shines most bright, most beautiful; but it is separated from us by so great a distance as to be raised above our investigations as above the storms and clouds of earth."

Stirling took off the reading glasses and lay in the resultant pitch darkness. Judge Latham had marked many passages like that in the strange collection of books that made up his library. In the five months that had passed since his attempt to escape, Stirling had spent most of his spare time flicking through the micro-library, hoping to find that the judge had slipped the missing frames from the encyclopedia into some other volume. All he had achieved was the discovery that Latham had a mystical streak in his nature, and in choosing the Ile as the place to die had been pursuing a vision, perhaps one more vivid than that which had activated both Johnny and himself. The judge had even written one quotation on the inside of the micro-library's lid:

"Great Spirit, give to me a heaven not so large as yours but large enough for me."

Its significance escaped Stirling, but he did not feel qualified to criticise another man for overlaying the hard reality of the Ile with the colours of his own dreams. He pulled the sleeping bag up to his chin and waited for sleep. Although winter had come early to Heaven that year, the shell field and a minimal amount of under-soil heating had kept the temperature to reasonable levels. The snow clouds crowded by, far below the raft, in great grey rivers, while the villagers lived in the thin, pure sunlight of a faded water-colour.

Stirling now knew almost everybody in the community and admitted to himself that he had begun to look like the other villagers. At his most conservative estimate, he had lost twenty kilos in weight, and felt as though he could have run the full length of the Ile. His skin had darkened to the colour of polished teak, and his stubble had developed into a rakish, seignorial-looking beard. But underneath his new, piratical exterior, his early instinctive desire to get off the Ile had crystalised into a diamond-hard determination, which was with him every second of every day. In his dreams he walked city streets, drinking in the sights and sounds of the culture which had spawned him – but sleep was not always easily achieved.

Stirling had been lying in darkness for an indeterminate time when he became aware of distant voices rising and falling, like the sound of waves sifting shingle. Several people ran by the stockade, talking excitedly in breathless whispers. Recognising an unusual amount of activity for the time of night, Stirling got up again and crossed to the door. He waited until he heard more leisurely steps outside, then rattled the lashed door against its frame.

"What's going on out there?"

"Go back to bed, Vic," someone replied. "It's nothing to do with you."

"Will you tell me what's happening, or do I kick this door down?"

"Ah, it's nothing. Old man Latham has finally bought it. His daughter's having some kind of a fit back there."

Stirling went to his pack and took out the final cigarette he had been saving for some unspecified occasion. He puffed it into life and drew deeply; but the dry smoke ravaged his lungs and made him cough. And, when he had snuffed out the tiny orange spark, the night seemed very much darker than before.

Stirling was not allowed to attend the funeral, but he saw the party wind its way along the margin to the grass-covered bank of drifted dust which served the villagers as a graveyard. The bank, heaped against the eastern wall by air eddying through a configuration of larger tanks, was not long and was little more than a metre in depth at its maximum. Stirling had no idea how many people had died on the Ile, but he guessed their bodies were keeping each other pretty close company. The Great Spirit was seeing to it that Judge Latham's allotted heaven was not over-large.

While the straggling procession was returning a west-bound jet grumbled its way down through the sky, and the villagers dispersed into the background. Stirling returned to the work of repairing the nets used by the food-foraging teams.

An hour later, during the midday break, Melissa Latham came to the stockade where Stirling had been doing much of his work during the colder weather. He had not seen her, except at a distance, for several months and was surprised to realise how much of her already economical body had been pared away by the strain of tending her father. Her eyes looked bruised.

Stirling stood up. "I'm sorry . . ."

"He told me to give you this." She held out Latham's gold wristwatch.

"I couldn't take it."

"It's all right. It doesn't work, and the gold is meaningless."

"I don't mean that – I mean, it was your father's."

"I don't *need* it." Melissa looked at him with a new curiosity. "He made me promise you would have it."

"All right – thanks." Stirling accepted the watch and warmed its chilly metal in his hands. "I don't know how much it would mean to you at this moment, but when your father knew he was going to die he picked the place where he wanted to go . . . And I think he made a good personal choice."

"He told you he was ill before he came here?"

"Yes. You don't . . ."

"It happened afterwards. He could have been cured if he had been able to go back."

"Didn't he try?"

"No." Melissa sounded almost defiant.

87

"But that's . . ." Stirling searched for the right word, and found his vocabulary inadequate. "What are you going to do now?"

"Too soon . . . Too soon . . ." Her gaze flicked past him. Stirling looked around and saw Johnny Considine approaching, for once without his entourage. It was the first time in five months that he had come within speaking distance. His eyes were fixed on Latham's watch with a look of overt covetousness which Stirling found puzzling.

"Here, Johnny." Stirling offered him the watch. "I suppose I'm expected to render unto Caesar."

Johnny put out his hand, carefully wrapped Stirling's fingers around the watch, and squeezed down on them. He gave Stirling a stare of resentment from stranger's eyes, but did not speak. Stirling suddenly understood that the watch was a symbol, not in its physical reality, but in the giving of it by the judge.

Still without speaking, Johnny put his arm around Melissa's shoulders; and she allowed herself to be led away. When they were almost out of earshot Melissa said something in a low, angry voice. Johnny, glancing back once over his shoulder, answered her; and Stirling knew why he had been so silent when they were together. His voice was a thin, plaintive squawk which showed that the vocal prosthetic was rapidly failing. Johnny was destined to be a king who gave commands with his fingers.

Stirling put the watch in his pocket and returned to the nets. Second in importance only to the rule that nobody went back, was the villagers' law that the food supplies had to be gathered over the widest possible area. The foraging teams travelled the full width of the Ile and diffused their demands to escape the electronic musings of distant computers – and nets were necessary for transportation.

Stirling worked stolidly with the tough plastic strands, while his mind re-ran the brief encounter with his brother. Johnny had changed again, this time for the worse. His personality seemed to be imploding on itself, building up internal

88

pressures which would not be contained, like a fission-fusion bomb. The symptoms would not have been apparent to anyone else; but Stirling had read them hazing through Johnny's eyes like the wind patterns drifting on his striated kingdoms of grain. But what was eating into Johnny? Disillusionment with the Ile and the pettiness of his chieftainship? Imagined or real rejection by both Judge Latham and Melissa? That might explain his reaction to seeing Melissa hand Stirling a worthless watch.

The skin of Stirling's face prickled coldly, as though it had been dusted with ice particles.

A worthless watch!

He stood up, stretched casually, and made his way into the stockade. Just inside the doorway – where the light was still good – he stopped, took out the watch, and sprang open its case. Nothing, except its magnetic motor and escapement. He examined the plastic of the strap for stitching which might have been disturbed; but it was made of a single thickness. Again nothing. Breathing heavily with frustration, he studied the body of the watch for the second time. The face was a lamination of gold which could be lifted away from the backing plate. Stirling pried it up with his thumbnail and saw the imprisoned corner of a microfilm frame. He began to tremble.

Stirling waited four days before the right opportunity came. The big robots had become less active during the colder weather; but on two occasions one of them came right to the end of a strip near the village. Each time, there was another close by, and he decided to pass up the chance. He did not want to ride out on one of the yellow machines if the villagers were able to jump others close behind, because at the western end of the Ile there would be an eight-kilometre run to the elevator's head. Even with his new flat-bellied physique, Stirling had no desire to race that distance against a horde of ragged cheetahs without a substantial headstart. The best solution would have been to go along the western margin to the centre line before making his break; but his earlier escape attempt had barred that road.

On the afternoon of the fourth day, he was operating the crude press which made fuel briquettes from dried grass and roots when a robot advanced right to the end of its strip and halted. Sterile sunlight glinted on the spider legs as they moved solicitously beneath the turret; apparently they were preparing the open soil for next spring's planting.

Stirling surveyed the Ile cautiously and saw that the southeast corner was otherwise free of the robots. The village itself was gripped by the mid-afternoon somnolence. The sound of a woman singing mingled with the faint, regular hammering of a man working at the distant end. Thin plumes of smoke drifted up from the shielded cooking fires in the central area and mixed with the ever-present canopy of water vapour. Even the nameless midget who had been appointed to watch Stirling was not in evidence.

Suppressing the unpleasant idea that this might be a more elaborate, and final test of his trustworthiness, Stirling began walking towards the patiently grazing robot. During the four days' wait, he had tried to analyse Latham's motives for breaking the self-imposed pact with the villagers, the pact to which he had sacrificed his own life. His tentative conclusion was that the judge had intended him to bring Melissa with him, if Johnny had decided to take her by force and she had objected strenuously enough. But Stirling had seen neither of them since the morning after Latham's death, nor had he heard of any scenes of spectacular rapine. He had decided to go when the going was good – regardless of any concomitant feelings of guilt. Besides, there was always the risk something would go wrong.

From close up, the nearside bogey of the robot was reminiscent of a locomotive, with its massive steel wheels and profusion of cylinders and levers. The yellow-painted structure was covered by a beaded blanket of condensation, under which were ancient streaks of oil, hydraulic fluid, and the other liquids which coursed its plastic arteries. Resisting the urge to take a final look around – the familiar, furtive gesture which so often attracts attention where flagrantly unusual conduct has failed – Stirling climbed up the sweating metal until he had reached the level of the beam which spanned above the soil bed to the bogey on the opposite side. He walked along its broad, upper flange, still trying to maintain an air of nonchalance, until the complex bulk of the turret was beneath him. The lower flange of the beam carried the rails upon which the turret could travel the full width of the strip. Praying there was nothing there which would electrocute him, Stirling dropped down onto it through a flexible tangle of helical pipes, and crawled into the turret itself. He located the panel giving access to the robot's alarm-system relays and began releasing the stiff, spring-loaded catches. From the corner of his eye, he saw a small black figure dart away through the village.

The solution to his problem had been simple. In fact, he had been given a good clue during his first minutes on the Ile when a big robot had passed him at full speed. It had been heading for the point where he had dived into the bean rows to escape the scarecrow.

Along the 24-kilometre length of each soil bed was a sensory network designed to warn the robot of crop damage, at any point, by detecting cellulose particles emitted from crushed or broken stems. The network also monitored soil moisture in case a malfunction of the irrigation system should cause localised parching or flooding; but it was the former function which gave the villagers the power to control the robots. In retrospect, Stirling was able to piece together what had gone wrong with his first escape bid. While he had been slogging along the Ile on foot, someone had found Biquard and raised the alarm. The hunters had summoned a robot by smashing down some plants; then they mounted it and manipulated the alarm relay panel to make the big machine think there was trouble at the opposite end of the strip. The fretful monster had thundered off at 80 kilometres an hour to investigate, incidentally overtaking Stirling on the way.

In theory it was perfectly straightforward, but the catches of the access panel appeared not to have been disturbed for years and had been designed for robotic pincers anyway. Stirling had wasted a precious minute and torn the skin of his fingers, before the last clamp fell away. He glanced towards the village and saw men running, loping across the margin like black wolves. Some were carrying what seemed to be spears. He clawed at the panel and discovered it had bonded itself to the surrounding casing.

Down below him one figure outstripped all the others, and Stirling recognised it at once. Dix was moving over the tough grass at an incredible speed, more like the shadow of an aircraft than a man, and his pike mouth was agape, scooping in air. He was also carrying an automatic pistol.

Swearing in sudden panic, Stirling scrabbled at the panel's edges and felt it lift slightly. He worked his fingertips in and pulled the rectangle of thick plastic upwards, revealing orderly rows of miniature relays, each of which was covered by a transparent case. The spring clips of the end case defeated his bloodied fingers for a second, then the smooth plastic cover popped off. Stirling saw Dix leap onto the robot's bogey and swarm up it, seemingly without losing speed. He jabbed his finger down on the exposed relay, closing its contacts – and nothing happened.

He had chosen the wrong end of the relay banks. He had ordered the robot to go to the sector it was already in.

Stirling was wrestling the cover from the relay at the opposite end, when Dix appeared above him on the upper flange of the beam. Dix steadied himself, lower teeth bared, and levelled the automatic. Stirling skimmed the access panel at him – causing him to duck away – and at the same time drove his heel down through the relay covers, splintering the fragile plastic and closing half-a-dozen contacts at once. The big machine lurched into motion; and as Dix overbalanced down onto the turret, he windmilled his arms against the sky. Stirling brought up his right knee, catching the falling man in the small of the back and bouncing him clear of the turret for the long drop to the soil bed. Two alloy-tipped spears clattered off the metal behind Stirling; but the robot was quickly gaining speed, and the frantically running figures lost ground.

Stirling leaned back against the beam and sombrely watched them dwindle away into the distance. He had calculated that the robot, travelling at top speed, would travel the length of the Ile in eighteen minutes. This was very much better than leaving on foot, but it was such a spectacular form of departure that his headstart could also be measured in minutes. To be precise, it would be the number of minutes it took for the villagers to summon another robot and get it under manual control. Ten minutes would be a good lead to achieve under the conditions, and that was not much in the context of the eight-kilometre run waiting at the Ile's western end – especially if his pursuers had guns.

From his vantage point high on the speeding machine, Stirling could see the full spread of the Ile and the random scattering of the other robots. He kept watching to the north, across the bare brown strips, and was surprised to note that a good five minutes had passed before one of the yellow structures, which had been tilling close to the Ile's lateral axis, suddenly moved off in the direction of the village. Allowing two minutes turnaround time, he was going to have a lead of some fourteen minutes. He thought about the unexpected bonus for a moment before remembering that, in the absence of growing crops to be damaged, the villagers could summon a robot only by means of the flood-alarm system. It would have taken them some time to transport water to the end of a strip.

When he had manually tripped the relay which would ensure that the machine would travel right to the end of the strip, Stirling climbed around to the forward side of the beam and sat watching the transit area expand ahead of him. Beyond the Ile's western rim, blue vistas of distance opened up, and Stirling's wind-watered eyes picked out the ordered verticalities of the coastal conurbation standing out through the haze like a cut-out stage prop. The sun was setting redly in

93

the shady immensities beyond the towers, and already the automobiles on the lower street levels were using their lights. Looking at the flickering points of brilliance, Stirling felt a suddenly intensified yearning to be back there, snug and tight in his own slot in civilisation. *I can make it*, he thought in wonderment, *I could be back home tonight*. He felt an icy focus of anxiety grow in his stomach: after almost half a year in Heaven, it all seemed too good to be true.

At the end of the strip, the humming, vibrating machine slowed down and covered the last hundred metres at walking pace, while its baffled logic circuits exchanged arguments at the speed of light. Stirling waited his chance and sprang onto the raised transit area. Immediately, he was hit by the lower temperature; but he put his head down and began to run. The elevator terminal was almost eight kilometres away to the north, and there was no time to coddle protesting lungs.

As he ran, Stirling discovered there were irregularities in the Ile's shell field which permitted the ambient sub-zero temperatures outside to encroach a short distance at some points. This was the first evidence he had found of maintenance failure, and he wondered if the Food Technology Authority was beginning to win its battle against the Iles. The shell field generators would be expensive to replace, and perhaps the East Coast administration had been forced to curtail its spending.

Although the shield itself was invisible under normal conditions, the areas where it was weakest were easily identifiable by the thick coating of frost which lay over everything, and by the raw pain which tore his lungs and throat each time he passed through. Stirling ran on steadily, amazed at the sheer efficiency of his body now that it was unhampered by its former blanket of fat. In each new sector he entered, a bright red scarecrow sprang into life and pursued him with flailing arms and a fusillade of loud reports; but he had learned that they moved on their own track system and for that reason were easily avoided.

He kept glancing back over his right shoulder, waiting to see a robot travelling westwards at speed. As the minutes went by and the lighted gantries of the elevator head became visible far in front, Stirling began to relax. He had begun to feel more confident the last time too – just before the sky fell in on him – but this time he had figured many more of the angles. The distance he had run, coupled with the effect of the thinner air near the shell failures, began to tell on him, and he felt his legs slow down of their own accord. Stirling tried forcing them to move faster; but after all, a wheedling voice told him, he was further ahead than he had dared hope to be.

When he finally saw a robot speeding out of the dusk that was gathering in the east, Stirling realised that, once again, he had underestimated the villagers. The robot was in the wrong place! He had been glancing backwards for signs of pursuit; but this machine, which was perhaps eight kilometres out from the transit area, was thundering along a strip which ended half a kilometre ahead of him.

As geysers of dismay and anger fountained through his system, Stirling called upon suddenly available reserves of energy and discovered what it was like really to *run*. He experienced the sensation as a hunted animal experiences it. Skimming along over the frosted tracks, he saw that the robot was moving along a strip devoted to winter wheat. Somebody in the village had decided not to use the slower flood-alarm method of summoning a robot, and had run along the Ile's eastern margin to the area where crops were still growing. That way they had saved a lot of time and – great cymbals of panic crashed in Stirling's ears – would be only a matter of metres behind their quarry when they leapt out, fresh and eager, onto the transit area.

He tried to run faster, but his body had reached realms of exhaustion in which adrenalin was unable to perform its ancient duties. Beyond the reach of biological expedients, only human will kept Stirling's arms and legs pumping in the desperate rhythms of flight. He heard his breath come and go in guttural shouts; his mouth filled with salt froth; and the horizons rocked uncontrollably about him. The distance between himself and the robot closed rapidly; he glimpsed dark figures poised along the beam; then he was past the point of intersection, with only seconds to spare. Shouts rang out close behind him as the ragged skirmishers sprang from their fantastic chariot.

*There's a long way to go yet before you reach the monitor cameras at the elevator head. You'll never make it – give up now before you burst your heart.*

The voice in his head seemed to be that of a friend who genuinely loved him, but Stirling ignored it. He tried to find some miraculous loophole in the laws of body chemistry which would allow him to go faster, but knew at last that he had failed. A short spear skipped past him like a furious reptile; then something had chopped across his ankles. He fell forward, rolling and slithering, as his precious momentum squandered itself.

Stirling sensed, rather than saw, the villagers overtake him. Rough hands turned him over . . . Dark figures loomed against the sky . . . A knife was raised and began its downward curve . . .

"Leave that man alone!"

Stirling barely heard the voice amid the roar of the blood torrents in his own system, but he saw the villagers freeze into black statues. He turned his head towards the voice and saw men running from the direction of the elevator head.

Men in the white uniforms of the Food Technology Authority.

## Chapter Eleven

Jepson Lomax was a pale round-faced man, with liver-coloured lips and clammy hands which he rubbed continually with a lime handkerchief. Each time he touched his desk, condensation left a ghostly handprint which slowly shrank to nothing as its moisture evaporated into the air of his office. He threw Stirling's press card into a wire tray and walked to the window. He moved like a much bigger and older man.

"Fantastic view, isn't it? All that open space. I've been on FTA ocean processing stations most of my working life; so I'm used to distant horizons. That's one of the reasons I got this job. But it's not the same at sea. It isn't the same as looking at wide open land." Lomax waved at the view beyond his window. "Nothing's the same as that."

Stirling nodded slowly. Beyond the double glazing, the broad acres of Heaven vapoured introspectively in the morning sun, ruled strips tapering into hazy distance. To Stirling, it all looked strangely unreal. He was still trying to find his mental feet in the new situation, and nothing seemed quite solid or real any longer. Especially this prefabricated office building which had been erected at the elevator head and peopled by comfortable, smoothly shaven FTA executives in white uniforms.

"I might as well be frank with you, Mr Stirling." Lomax mopped his palms mechanically. "I've had a couple of very unpleasant shocks during the past twenty-four hours. To discover a bunch of . . . hoboes on this Ile was bad enough. But the fact that you, a newspaperman, got onto them first makes things all the more difficult for me."

"I don't understand."

"Well, it means we may not be able to let you go." Lomax smiled an apology, whose obvious insincerity made it a threat. "You see, we don't want to draw attention to our presence here . . . So it would hardly be advisable for me to release a reporter with one of the most sensational stories of the century.

"You do see my point of view, don't you?"

Stirling stood up angrily. "Listen, I'm grateful to you for saving my life. But I don't see what right you have to even think about keeping me here against my will. The FTA has no power to . . ."

"Correction, Mr Stirling." Lomax stretched his brown lips in another formal smile. "You forget how long you've been . . . shall we say, out of touch? Last month both coastal administrations approved a rationalisation programme which brought the Iles under the Authority's direct control."

"All right, so Hodder finally got the Iles in his pocket. Where does that leave me?"

"It leaves you in the middle of a quiet revolution, Mr Stirling. Weren't you surprised to find us here?"

"I was coming to that."

"I'll bring it to you. Do you know what percentage of the country's food supply comes from the Iles?"

"I don't know. Five? No, I guess that's too high. One or two?"

"Point oh-oh-two."

Stirling looked out at Heaven's blurred horizons in disbelief. "But that's only . . ."

"Not worth taking into consideration, is it? And do you know how much it costs to produce a kilo of incomplete protein on the Iles, compared with extracting a kilo of whole protein from the ocean?" A look of expectancy appeared on Lomax's round face; and Stirling, realising he was taking part in a set piece, became irritated.

"All I want to know is, what makes you think you can keep me here?"

Lomax frowned. "The Iles are finished, Mr Stirling. The

only useful function left to them is to provide living space. That's what we need more than a few vegetables right now."

Stirling suddenly saw the light. "Do you mind if I make a wild guess about what you're going to say next? I imagine that, as the FTA controls these choice pieces of real estate, it has also selected the tenants. Right?"

Lomax nodded, still looking amused.

"And who would it choose but its own executives? If Hodder's plans work out, there's going to be a kind of technocracy on both coasts, with the FTA on top . . . And the Iles will become glorified penthouses for Hodder and his puppets."

"I *knew* you would understand why we can't let you go, Mr Stirling. Under the new legislation there's nothing really illegal about what we're doing here, but it will take the great American public some time to get used to the idea. Our public relations agency has barely got started on the job and – with the congressional elections coming up soon – it could be inconvenient for the Authority if you were to talk to the wrong people."

"I don't see what you're worrying about," Stirling said bitterly. "Your so-called Press Council would block everything I wrote. I'm one of their best customers."

"You journalists become too wrapped up in the press." Lomax began drawing the pale green handkerchief between each of his fingers in turn. "You forget about things like whispering campaigns, Mr Stirling. Public opinion was a potent electioneering weapon long before newspapers were invented.

"The Authority insists on you remaining here as its guest for the time being. But relax . . . It won't be for very long."

*How right you are*, Stirling thought. He walked to the window and looked out to the spot where work crews were unloading earth-moving equipment from the elevator cars. *How right you are.*

Stirling found he had been given complete freedom of movement within the building which – when he thought it over – was much better treatment than he might have expected. Lomax and a couple of FTA security men had questioned him closely after dragging him into the safety of their office block; but Stirling had stuck to his story of coming to the Ile as a reporter in search of an unusual scoop. His instinctive dislike for anyone connected with the FTA had led him to keep quiet about Johnny and to be vague about the number of people in the village.

Finally, Lomax accepted him at face value; and Stirling got the impression the FTA thought the four men they had captured with him represented the bulk of the Ile's unofficial colony. He was content to leave it that way. When the new landlords unexpectedly encountered an army of two hundred shabby guerrillas, their cloak of secrecy was likely to come apart at the seams.

Once free of Lomax, Stirling explored the single-storey building. Drafting computers had been set up in some of the rooms, and men in FTA whites were everywhere. Stirling noticed that, in contrast to most citizens of the Compression, the men were tanned; and he guessed they had worked on the processing stations along the coast. That would make them good material for the Ile: anybody who had been used to seascapes would adapt more easily. He ambled around, ignoring the curious stares from the office workers, until he found the wing which was being used as a temporary prison. The four captured villagers sat disconsolately behind a superglass partition. Stirling surveyed their faces and satisfied himself Johnny was not there; then he noticed the men's movements were limited by webs of silvery streamers clinging around their limbs.

"What's that stuff?"

The square-faced security man on guard looked coldly at Stirling, but he answered. "We used blotch guns on those guys. Good thing for you we had 'em too."

"I appreciate it. Is that a blotch gun?" He pointed at the bulbous weapon of grey metal clipped to the guard's belt.

"Yeah. Best yet for security work . . . Better range than the old bolas guns we used to have, and that solder wraps 'em up but good."

100

"That's progress for you."

Stirling stared through the superglass at the villagers. Yesterday they had tried to kill him; today he bore them no grudge. All the rules had been changed. One of the villagers, his lips moving silently behind the screen, looked up, recognised Stirling, and pointed him out to the others. The four faces looked strangely alike: dark-skinned, bearded, hunted, and trapped. Stirling knew none of them by name, and guessed they had been four nonentities who happened to find themselves in the wrong place at the wrong time.

He moved on and picked a convenient window from which to watch the reconstruction teams at work. They had begun spreading along two strips, dozing the soil into tumbled brown heaps, pouring plastic floors, and erecting wall panels. Beyond the new buildings loomed the yellow structure of an agricultural robot, strangely canted; and showers of sparks fountained up around it from cutting machines. The robot looked oddly dignified in death, and Stirling felt something like regret.

The first battle of International Land Extension, US 23, took place three days later.

An unofficial survey team of three men had headed out across the Ile early in the afternoon, partly to see the territory for themselves, partly for the pleasure of the ride. Their negative-gravity sled was set to travel about a metre above the level of the soil beds, but it moved with a faint undulating motion due to the interaction of its own field with the beam fields of the Ile's substructure. From his vantage point, Stirling saw the men laugh as they discovered the newly arrived sled's tendency to behave like a roller coaster. He watched the party disappear into the east and wondered, uneasily, how long it would be before the village was discovered. The sled reappeared an hour later, travelling at top speed, rising and falling like a swallow in its skimming flight. Two of the men were slumped in their seats, and their white overalls were dappled with crimson. The report which filtered down to Stirling was that

101

they had seen a solitary figure moving in the eastern margin, had tried to round him up, and found themselves right in the middle of the village. Only the sled's impressive acceleration had got them back out of it – and two of the survey team had serious knife wounds.

An hour after the sled's return, Lomax appeared in the room which he had allocated to Stirling. His brown lips were twitching with anger.

"I expected no cooperation from those four . . . animals we caught with you, but I thought you were an impartial observer, Stirling."

"I don't get you." Stirling met his gaze squarely.

"You must have known how many of these people there were on the Ile, but you didn't tell me. Why not?"

Stirling shook his head. The question was a difficult one, even for him. He was opposed to Hodder and the idea of the nation's sole food supplier acquiring all the powers of government, but he had never been the type to sacrifice his own interests to a political ideal. Had he some more personal, deeply buried motive for wanting the whole Ile business to blow up in everybody's faces?

"All right, don't answer," Lomax snapped thinly. "But remember, I'm holding you responsible for the lives of those two men. I am also confining you to this room until the Authority decides what action to take against you. Don't try to leave."

Stirling gave a mock salute as Lomax went out. He sat down on the edge of his folding bed and wished that half a year in Heaven had not ruined his taste for a cigarette.

Within a matter of hours FTA reinforcements began to arrive at the elevator head. Eight negative-gravity sleds fitted with armoured bubbles of superglass drifted off the cars, waltzing slightly, nudging each other's bumper rings. With each sled was a crew of FTA security men carrying blotch guns and an assortment of more conventional weapons.

Stirling watched the little flotilla course off over the Ile's gravity gradients in the pewter light of dawn. The first sortie

102

lasted three hours and, he learned later, was an almost complete failure due to the fact that the security men were unable to find the village. On the second sortie, the unharmed member of the original hapless trio led the way; and they found the village, but no villagers.

At that point, Lomax began to lose interest; he realised that his building programme was free to carry on for as long as it took to reach the eastern end of the Ile and that by that time, the problem of the villagers would have sorted itself out. The expeditions became sporadic, almost casual affairs which seemed to be governed by how restless or adventurous the security men felt on any particular day. As the prospect of an imminent explosion began to dwindle, Stirling began to realise he really was – once more – a prisoner, and his sentence would last for perhaps two years. He had an unsatisfactory interview with Lomax at which he learned that the two wounded men would live and that the FTA was still determined to keep Stirling confined to his room. Two armed security men escorted him back to his quarters; and the painstaking way in which they remained beyond the range of fists, but inside the effective radius of a blotch gun made Stirling wonder, strickenly, if he *was* going to be cooped up for the foreseeable future.

A few hours later, one of the patrols accidentally made contact and returned with two prisoners. One of them died on the sled ride back to the elevator head.

The other was Melissa Latham.

"All right, Stirling, outside." The security guard held open the door of Stirling's room and waved him out into the corridor with drawn blotch gun.

"What's happening?" Stirling left his vantage point at the window.

"Mr Lomax has finished talking to that woman we brought in, and he's giving her your room until we ship the lot of you downstairs."

"So where do I go?"

"In with your buddies, of course. If they try to knife you again, just sing out. I'm a light sleeper."

103

"You're such a comfort, Milburn." Stirling reluctantly gathered up his jacket and walked out ahead of the guard. Melissa! How had she managed to get caught? Why did it have to be her? How many forces were working to prevent him going back?

Part way along the narrow corridor, a door opened in front of him, and Melissa was ushered out of an office by Lomax. He was smiling behind her; and his fingers traced the contours of her shoulders – not quite touching the skin – as he directed her to Stirling's old room. Melissa's flat-planed face was pale, masked with dust. It makes no difference, he thought. Her eyes widened for an instant as she saw Stirling, and she tried unsuccessfully to smile. "It makes no difference," he told himself, but the words came out differently.

"What do you think you're doing, Lomax? You can't keep her here."

"I don't intend to," Lomax replied pleasantly. "The Authority has arranged new quarters down below for you and all other trespassers we catch. I'm sending you down in the morning."

Stirling saw a pulse begin to flicker in Melissa's throat, and he tried to visualise her reactions to being buried in a Compression prison. He had a strong conviction that she would, quite simply, die.

"Keep moving, big man," Milburn said from behind. Stirling glanced back and saw that the guard had not forgotten the basic theory of firearms: when you have a weapon which acts at a distance, don't throw away your advantage by going up close. If Stirling tried anything, Milburn would get off at least one shot, and apparently it was not necessary to be very accurate with a blotch gun. I'm sorry, Melissa, he thought. I hope this doesn't hurt too much.

He put his hand on Melissa's arm, as if to sympathise with her, then tightened his grasp, and jerked hard. Melissa was lifted right off her feet and hurled towards Milburn. There was a vicious *splat* as the guard fired instinctively; and Stirling saw an octopus of silvery metal wrap itself around Melissa binding

104

her instantly into a rigid human spindle. Then he was past her, pushing the gun aside with one hand and pile-driving Milburn down onto his knees with the other. Stirling snatched the gun and turned around in time to see Lomax sprint towards his office door. He fired the unfamiliar weapon twice and saw Lomax topple sideways, wrapped up like a Christmas present. Melissa had gone down too; so Stirling lifted her under his left arm and ran for the outer door. Nobody got in his way, and in less than ten seconds he was outside in the cool darkness. The eight large negative-gravity sleds and the two smaller ones were parked in a neat row beside the entrance. Stirling unceremoniously dumped Melissa into a small one, then ran along the line firing the blotch gun into the controls of the other nine. The gun felt noticeably lighter when he had finished, but nobody was going to come after him that night – unless they came on foot.

He ran back to the sled in which Melissa lay, leaped in, and boosted the tiny craft off towards the east in a prolonged burst of acceleration which threatened to drag him back from the controls. The lighted windows and frantically running figures of the FTA headquarters shrank abruptly, like a scene on a deflated balloon.

Stirling felt a surge of pleasure, then he remembered there was nowhere to run to in the darkness that lay ahead. Nowhere, except the village.

## Chapter Twelve

In the first light of morning, Stirling examined the effects of the blotch gun charge which had caught Melissa. There was a hand-sized blob of the strange metal at her waist, where she had been hit; and rigid tentacles radiating from it lapped around body and limbs. He discovered that the streamers could be uncoiled individually if he held them tightly and was careful not to let them snap back. The blotch gun's efficacy depended on trussing the victim so securely that he was unable to exert any leverage to free himself. The only drawback to his releasing Melissa was a social one: the fast-moving tentacles had traversed every part of her body.

"Perhaps," Stirling said as he worked to separate metal, clothing, and skin, "I should leave your arms till the end. This sort of thing always earns me a slap on the face."

Melissa looked up at him with a wickedness he had not expected. "You mean this is the way you usually get your women?"

"I don't need to use force," he said haughtily. "Sometimes I just sneak up from behind and chloroform them."

Melissa laughed easily, seemingly at peace with her world, now that she was going back to the village. Stirling was amazed at her inability to understand that the Ile, as she and the other villagers knew it, was virtually a thing of the past. The vacation in the sky was drawing to a close. He stood up and cautiously looked out of the nest of tall winter wheat in which the sled was lying. There was no sign of pursuit; but he thought he could detect figures moving on the roof of the Ile's central power station projecting up out of the haze several kilometres behind.

"Lomax seems to have taken over the power station," he said. "They really mean business, Melissa. How many months or weeks does Johnny think you'll be able to hang on now?"

"Victor," she replied, using his name for the first time, "Johnny didn't take over the village by muscle power alone. I know Dad didn't like him; but he has qualities which Dad might have recognised if he hadn't been growing timid and afraid towards the end."

"But what can he do when a thing like this is sprung on him?"

"That's the point. It wasn't sprung on him. Johnny knew about those men the first day they arrived a month ago to build their headquarters. He's been making plans – and I think you ruined them by breaking away just when you did."

Stirling felt swamped. "Plans! Have you been up here so long you've forgotten what you're up against? The Food Technology Authority, the Government, and the people of the United States – that's what you're up against. What plan could compensate for odds of a million to one against you?"

Melissa looked unperturbed. "Johnny says it isn't force that counts – it's leverage."

"Come on," Stirling said heavily. "We'd better leave this thing and go on to the village on foot."

It was mid-morning when they neared the village, but there was no sign of the thin columns of smoke from the central cooking fires. Stirling was scanning the grass-shrouded tank structures on either side as they reached the area representing the community's northern limits. Even his practised eye could detect no life; and he decided the villagers had moved out, or were better at concealment than he had realised.

"I thought we had seen the last of you," a voice said from behind.

Stirling spun around and saw Paddy walking a few paces to the rear. He was carrying a rusted, but obviously still functional, pistol in one brown hand.

"Put that thing away," Melissa said quickly. "You can tell Johnny he'd have seen the last of *me* if Vic hadn't been there."

Paddy shrugged. "You tell him. He doesn't listen to me much."

When Stirling was shepherded into the Council's hut, it looked pretty much as it did the first night he had seen it. The same faintly burning glow-globe – brought by some thoughtful rebel many years earlier – was casting a sickly light over the matted walls. Johnny was, as usual, stripped to the waist, and his eyes burned at Stirling through reddened rims. He looked like a human time bomb.

"I hear you brought Melissa back. Is she all right?"

Stirling almost winced as he heard the reedy caricature of a voice which issued from the prosthetic at Johnny's throat. He nodded.

"For that much, thanks."

Stirling felt a pang of guilt which prompted him to explain. "I like Melissa. I wasn't doing you any favours, Johnny."

"You weren't doing me any favours." Johnny laughed. "Oh, brother!"

Stirling allowed some time to pass in silence to give the emotional potentials a chance to subside. "Listen, Johnny. I'm truly sorry about all this, but isn't it time you woke up? I dislike the FTA as much as you do – if for different reasons – but you're fighting them the wrong way."

"How would you do it?"

"With publicity. The Authority has taken a risk by moving into the Iles with the elections coming up this year, and they didn't expect to find anybody already in residence. That's your lever against Lomax and the others. Make enough noise and you'll tear down the walls of Jericho."

Johnny traced patterns in the dust at his feet. "How about a radio broadcast from the Ile direct to everybody in the States?"

"Ideal – but how would you do it?"

"From the power station."

"You'd never get near it. Lomax has men all over it, and there's no cover anywhere around."

"Yeah. He has *now*. Before you gave the whole show away

there was no . . . Anyway, there is still a way we can get in. Will you help? I need at least ten men."

"Ten?" Stirling began to feel uneasy. "But you've over a hundred here already. Why do you need another volunteer?"

Johnny looked up, smiling crookedly, and Stirling felt a sensation which had not troubled him in months – an icy awareness of grey clouds prowling beneath his feet.

"Johnny, you're not . . ."

A woman screamed outside, and the sound was choked off by the angry rattle of machine rifles. Stirling and Johnny dived for the door. They found Paddy kneeling in the grass, hands holding his stomach, while deltas of blood coursed over his knuckles. West of the village four of the large sleds were shuttling just above soil bed level, and gunners on board them sprayed everything in sight.

Stirling lay prone in the long grass and watched the big sleds waltz and skid across the sky as their rifles searched through the village by filling the air with howling ricochets. It took less than three minutes for the gunners to empty their magazines; but time itself seemed to have been shocked into immobility. When the sleds finally skimmed away on full boost, silence came down hard for a few seconds; then, somewhere in the distance, a child began to cry. Johnny jumped to his feet and went to Paddy, who had fallen on one side.

"He's dead," Johnny said as Stirling approached. Something had added a new degree of distortion to his voice, beyond what the failing prosthethic could do. "He didn't even like me."

"The bastards," Stirling whispered in disbelief. "The dirty bastards."

"Well, how about it, big brother? Do we hit the power station?"

Stirling looked at the high eastern wall of the Ile, beyond which the invisible wind-rivers ran free, and his mouth went dry. "Is that the only way?"

"That's the only way, big brother. Over and under."

*

They waited until the following morning and set off at first light to cover the maximum distance before dark.

Stirling climbed the crude ladder which had been raised in the lee of a water tank where it could not be seen by FTA observers using binoculars. At the top he looked down once. Far below him lay arctic kingdoms of tumbled clouds, and beyond that again – visible through ragged tears in the vapour fabric – the grey Atlantic waited implacably. Microscopic ships trailed their miniature white chevrons through the close-packed corrugations of ocean waves.

Stirling wrenched his eyes away from the aerial immensities, and concentrated on the knotted rope which snaked down the outer side of the wall. Johnny had gone down first, while the rope was swinging free at the bottom end, and had tied it to the Ile's substructure. Heedless of how ungainly he might look to the men behind, Stirling rolled carefully over the metallic parapet and began working his way down the rope. The cold sliced into him immediately, in spite of the extra layers of clothing. At the bottom end he found himself looking into an incredible, upside-down landscape of massive, ice-encrusted lattice girders. Their multiple triangulations spanned the bays between the beams of the Ile's main grid, which carried in its boxy thickness the stolid, patient negative-gravity units. Johnny was straddling the broad back of the outer main tie, his hard body masked by heavy clothing, straps, and coils of rope. And, five kilometres under his feet, the grey Atlantic still waited implacably.

Transferring his weight from the rope to the main tie gave Stirling one bad moment; then he was sitting behind Johnny, listening to the lowing of the wind. He soon discovered that normal consciousness was impossible under the hideously alien circumstances. As the other eight members of the party came down the rope, Stirling concentrated on shrinking his radius of perception until the only real things in the universe were his own body and the narrow highway of icy metal underneath.

Johnny gave a signal and, still straddling the main tie, began pulling himself along towards the intersection of the nearest longitudinal lattice girder. Stirling and the others jockeyed along behind him like children playing a dangerous game. At the juncture it was necessary to stand up and edge round a massive vertical member to get onto the new tie. While trusting his life to the grip of numbed fingers on glassy metal, Stirling vowed to be deliriously happy twenty-four hours a day when he got back into the Compression. Johnny kept moving on ahead, tirelessly dragging himself along by his arms. In the line behind him, Stirling heard Dix swearing monotonously as the physical strain built up. Dix had survived his fall from the robot's turret – apparently without injury – but on learning that Stirling had been accepted as an equal member of the raiding party, he had relapsed into a watchful silence. The group's painful progress was slowed down even further when they encountered huge nodes, where structural members intersected in three planes. It had taken them over an hour to travel half a kilometre when Johnny signalled the others to catch up. He moved a little way along a lateral tie, and the villagers formed a silent audience on the nightmarish cross-roads.

"It's getting warmer. There's less ice this far in from the edge." The wind noises made it difficult to hear the ventriloquist's falsetto to which Johnny's voice had been reduced. "At this rate it'll take us a couple of days to reach the power plant, and we'll be finished when we do make it."

"So what do we do?"

"We walk. Just like we'd do up top. That way we can reach the plant before dark."

Before anybody had time to protest, Johnny stood up, stepped confidently across onto the longitudinal tie, and walked along it by leaning slightly into the north wind. Feeling grey and old, Stirling followed him, while he told himself that the slowly shifting masses far below might seem like clouds. But that was impossible because everybody knew the sky was always above your head, not ever licking around your heels. Somehow he managed to keep putting one foot past the other,

111

until the act of leaning on the wind – at an unconsciously computed angle which balanced the lateral pressure of air streams against the lethal yearnings of Mother Earth – became an automatic process. And, even at the faster rate of travel, it was dusk when they neared the downward-projecting hulk of the Ile's central power house.

They had a light supper of wheat cakes and water, then lashed themselves in sitting positions against vertical struts to wait out the long night. Stirling finally went to sleep, with his eyes fixed on the softly flickering lights of Newburyport glimmering through the indigo haze that lay to the west.

The power station had one door which could be reached from the underside. It was there for the benefit of the human maintenance crew who took a trip up to the Ile once every ten years to renew the fuel cartridges in its closed-system reactor. The trouble was that the crew always arrived in a seven-metre-square raft which fitted snugly into a docking area adjoining the door. A space had been left for it in the Ile's structure –which meant the villagers found themselves staring at the rectangular door across a dismaying void filled with ocean-reflected light. The door was fitted with a conventional handle and lock which had a ghastly incongruity, when five kilometres of nothing waited at the threshold.

Johnny worked his way around the docking bay to the power station's streaming wall, tied a rope to a vertical strut, and went right round the opening again to the opposite side. When he also tied the rope there, it spanned the gap a short distance out from the wall and on a level a metre from the top of the door. He repeated the operation again, working lower down, creating what might have been regarded as a bridge by a very desperate man.

"Neat," Stirling shouted. "But what about the lock?"

"My job," said a small man called Borges, who was sitting close to Stirling. "That one's a pushover – I can tell from here. I don't know why they bothered in the first place. I mean, nobody's likely to break into a place like . . . Well, it isn't much of a lock."

"That's the way I lose most of my arguments too," Stirling said sympathetically. "Good luck."

"I got it already. I don't weigh much; so that rope isn't likely to snap under my feet." Borges edged his way around the docking bay to where Johnny was standing. He hesitated for a moment, whispered something to himself, then raised his arms while Johnny tied a third rope around his chest to act as a lifeline. With a final and strangely shamefaced grin at the other villagers, Borges got into the plastic ropes, slid his feet along the lower, and held onto the higher one by twining both arms around it. The ropes bore his weight with very little sagging; but Stirling had learned they were woven from the high-tensile plastic used in the agricultural robots' control lines. At the door Borges took some fine tools from his pouch and went to work on the lock. Two minutes later he cautiously tried the handle, nodded, and came back along the ropes. Pearly morning light poured upwards around him.

"I told you I was lucky," he said as he found his place beside Stirling again.

Four of the party were equipped with pistols – which apparently had been brought to the Ile many years earlier by rebels, who were taking no chances about what they would find. The weapons had been absorbed into a communal armoury and were being carried on the raid by Johnny, Dix, and two other Council members: a narrow-shouldered, balding man called Forsythe, and a muscular Chinese known as Theodore. These four were to go in first, followed by the other villagers armed with knives and stubby spears. Stirling, who had not been given a weapon, was to be last into the station.

Johnny edged his way along the ropes, tried the door handle, pulled it open, and vanished into the darkness inside. Dix followed, then Forsythe and Theodore. Stirling listened intently, wondering if Lomax had any men right in the station and not merely camped out on the roof. There was a delay while the advance party sized up their immediate surroundings; then the door opened and Theodore signalled the others to come on. Four men went along the ropes one at a time and scrambled in through the door. Only Borges and Stirling remained behind. *If I were Lomax*, Stirling thought uneasily, *I would put my men inside*.

"Well, here goes." Borges was still grimacing with relief at having got back safely from his first trip across the void. He went carefully along the ropes and was almost at the door when muffled gunfire made itself heard above the wind. There were several separate shots, followed by the continuous thunder of an automatic weapon. Borges froze, and his face, a contorted mask of shock, turned back to Stirling.

"Don't stop," Stirling shouted. "Get inside."

Borges shook his head and began slithering back the way he had come. The automatic weapon sounded again, metal-tongued holes appeared in the sheeting of the door, and the door itself abruptly burst open as a body hit it from the inside. The swinging edge jerked the ropes away from the wall, taking the lower one out from under Borges' feet. He fell silently, pedalling his legs like a man running for his life, shrinking into a frantic manikin which was swallowed by the impassive clouds. Stirling snatched his own soul back from a vicarious dive into eternity and strung his body into the vibrating ropes. The rational part of his mind immediately dissociated itself from the venture, and he moved mechanically, hardly aware of the significance of the drifting white and grey masses below. He clawed open the door, threw himself into the opening, and sprawled across the body that lay just inside. It was wearing a white FTA uniform.

Stirling looked up and saw Dix standing a few feet away with an automatic rifle cradled on his hip. His lower teeth were displayed in an inhuman grin, and he kept the gun pointing at Stirling's face. Stirling was beginning to feel hopelessly afraid when there was a sound of running feet, and Johnny and Theodore appeared from behind a screen of heavily shielded cables.

"All clear up top," Johnny said. "I see you got one."

114

"Yeah." Dix nodded complacently. "I got one."

"Two," Stirling corrected. "Borges was just outside the door when you decided to have your bit of fun. You got two." He kept his eyes fixed on Johnny's as he spoke, and saw them cloud momentarily with pain and doubt.

"I had to do it, Jaycee," Dix said sullenly. "That guy came at me like a crazy man."

"He must have been a crazy man." Stirling got to his feet. "Considering you had his gun."

Johnny hesitated, fighting some lonely battle far inside himself; then he shrugged and turned away, avoiding Stirling's eyes.

"Why are you standing about?" Johnny's voice filled Stirling with a dismayed sadness. "The world's waiting to hear from us."

## Chapter Thirteen

There was very little free space anywhere in the station's four floors, but the FTA men had managed to find enough room on the top level to set up a kind of field camp. Just inside the rarely used entrance were three portable beds, chairs and a small table, and a communications set. A hatch, which had been cut in the roof, led to a nest of two heavy machine guns and a modern rad-rifle.

The raid had gone better than the attackers might have expected. Apart from the loss of Borges, the only casualty among the villagers was Forsythe, who had been kicked in the eye and almost blinded while going through to the roof. Of the four FTA men who had been in the station, one was dead – at the hands of Dix – and another had been shot in the knee. Johnny permitted the two remaining men to put their wounded comrade on a negative-gravity sled and fly him back to the elevator head. They had gone gratefully, with curious looks at the bearded viking, whose voice was a thin squawk issuing from a tarnished medallion at his throat.

In the meantime, Theodore, who was the party's nearest approach to an electronics expert, had been examining the communications set. Johnny sat down on a bed and began removing the extra clothing he had put on for the raid.

"What's the range of that thing?"

Theodore looked up from the set. "I'm out of touch, Jaycee. Can't say for sure."

"Will it reach the coast?"

"Which one?"

"What do you mean which one? The East Coast, of course. If I use that thing, will they hear me in Newburyport?"

"Sure thing, Jaycee. They'll be able to see you too."

"All right, fix it up for me. I want to talk now."

"Johnny." Stirling had been leaning against a wall, with unfocused eyes watching Borges fall into the clouds. "Do you want to block the channels right now? Lomax could come through at any minute, and it might be best to straighten him out first."

Johnny raised his eyebrows. "I don't think that would be too bright. If Lomax gets an idea of what we're planning, he'll do anything to stop us. He might have equipment there which could jam this set. Right, Theo?"

Theodore nodded; and Stirling realised he had been nursing a tiny, illogical hope that, somehow, he would succeed in escaping from the nightmare and get off the Ile with his anonymity still intact. But once the story became public, there would be an explosion which, as well as harming the FTA, would permanently alter the lives of all the men concerned. He could never again become Vic Stirling, the strolling reporter, the man whose only concern in life was keeping it at arm's length. All the wordage he had written against the FTA, all the anger he had expressed, none of it had ever touched another human being; and at last he understood why. He had been playing games and now – through blind chance – had strayed into the big league, where there was no second-guessing and the umpire's decision was very, very final.

Johnny walked over to the communications set. "How about wavelength? Who am I going to talk to?"

"How about using a police wavelength, Jaycee? That should stir things up for a start – and you get a lot of nosy characters listening in as well." Theodore spoke with the kind of patient, manufactured enthusiasm the villagers often used when addressing Johnny.

"That'll do. Set it up."

Johnny positioned himself in front of the set's console and began to talk, without hesitation or any signs of self-consciousness about either his ridiculous voice or the equally unlikely context of his message. He began by identifying

117

himself by name and former address: John Considine, Fam-apt 126–46, Flat-block 353, Res-area 93N–54W. As he reeled off the string of figures, Johnny's eyes met Stirling's for an instant, and their minds vaulted into realms beyond normal communication. *I always think a good address is* so *important, don't you?* But Stirling got a depressing intuition that this was the last real contact he and his brother would make.

Speaking calmly but quickly, Johnny stated where he was speaking from and, at Theodore's instigation, invited listeners with direction-finding equipment to check his bearing. He went on to say he was an eyewitness to the destruction of crops by FTA men who were building living quarters on the Ile, and that his statement would be verified by a reporter from the *Newburyport Record*, who was also present. Stirling took his place at the set and confirmed everything Johnny had said; he also added that the FTA had used machine guns in an effort to prevent their activities being brought to the attention of the American public.

He had barely finished speaking when Theodore picked up an incoming call and threw the picture onto the set's main screen. Stirling recognised the pale, round face, and sliced-liver lips of Jepson Lomax.

"Stirling!" Lomax leaned forward until the camera distorted his features. "You've brought yourself some real trouble this time. It may interest you to know that your name has gone up to Mr Hodder himself, and that . . ."

"It may interest *you*," Stirling interrupted, "to know that we've been using this communications set to broadcast direct to the East Coast."

"You've . . . what?"

"Starting any moment now, you're going to get a lot of calls about what's been going on here, Lomax. And I imagine your name has gone up to Mr Hodder himself along with mine." Stirling was surprised to discover how much he was enjoying the hour of self-immolation.

Lomax brought himself under control with an obvious effort. "I've given orders for you and the rest of those thugs to

118

be brought back to this building right away, Stirling. We'll see how insolent you can be in prison – if you can get back in one piece."

Stirling shrugged. "Tell your boys to hurry over. It would be best from our point of view if your gunners were doing their party piece when the first spectators arrive. Even a helicopter could get out here from the coast in less than five minutes; so they should be overhead any time now." He nodded at Theodore, who broke the connection, and Lomax's image went on a comet-ride into the spurious depths of the screen.

"Good stuff," Johnny said. "I think I'll appoint you my permanent press officer."

"It was good stuff, all right." Stirling could feel his elation begin to ebb. "I only hope Theodore had the set pushing it all out."

There was a movement at the hatch above their heads, and Dix called them up onto the roof. Stirling climbed up into the sunlight behind Johnny and peered towards the west to the spot where Dix was pointing. A flotilla of FTA sleds, rising and falling in flight, was coursing above the soil beds towards the station; but Stirling's gaze centred itself higher up.

Above the rim of the Ile, the crystal carapaces of three bubblecraft were glittering against the pale blue sky.

Johnny's next move filled Stirling with an even deeper sense of unease. He manhandled the rad-rifle down off the roof and used it to burn through the locks on the station's output master-switches. When the job was finished, Johnny had in his hands the power to drop International Land Extension, US 23, into the North Atlantic if he so desired.

Apart from not liking the implications of what Johnny was doing, Stirling was worried about what might happen if the rifle slipped at the wrong moment and burned through vital circuitry in another part of the station. He took his mind off it by sitting at the communications set and searching the wavebands to see how the various news-services were handling the story. The reaction had been almost immediate. On seeing the bubblecraft overhead, the FTA sleds had scampered back to headquarters to wait while Lomax assessed the new situation. And, in spite of the fact that it was illegal to overfly an Ile, the sky had been filled with assorted sizes and types of craft all morning – until the arrival of a squadron of army drift-ships had cleared the air. Even then, an occasional bubble filled with newsmen and photographers had been skimming in over the wall for a quick pass across the Ile. Watching the newscasts on the main screen, Stirling had felt a slight sense of dislocation at sitting inside the power station, yet seeing it from the machines passing above. Each time one of the machines passed by, the villagers manning the two guns remaining on the roof waved like excited children.

At first there had been some confusion in the news-stories: many stations had given the impression that the FTA had sent men onto the Ile simply to clear out newly discovered squatters. But Johnny's statement about the destruction of crops had burned in deep, and aerial shots of the building work in progress on the strips had begun to occupy most of the transmission time. Within two hours the major stations were using their political specialists on the story; and reports began to come in of Gordon Hodder, President of the FTA, and Lester B. Raddall, the East Coast Administrator, not being available for comment.

Stirling nodded in satisfaction – Hodder's propaganda machine was going to be faced with an impossible task trying to erase this incident from the public memory before the elections. Dealing the FTA a body blow had been almost too easy, Stirling thought, but what was going to happen next? Johnny was relaxed and confident, seemingly under the impression that Lomax had been his last enemy. He had already sent the FTA man a message that any further attempts to retake the power station would result in the lift energy for the whole western sector of the Ile being shut off at its source. Stirling was satisfied the threat would be effective against Lomax, but it would take more than that to restrain the entire FTA and the Government. If necessary, either one of them could – given a little time – set up ground-based equipment which would support the Ile long enough for a military action to be carried out against the villagers.

Late in the afternoon the communications set suddenly refused to pick up anything but audio and visual noise; and Stirling guessed Lomax, or someone higher up the pyramid, had given orders for the power station to be screened off. Johnny was unimpressed when told about it.

"When anybody who matters wants to get through to us, he will. Don't forget, they haven't heard my terms yet." He bit off a piece of wheat cake, washed it down with a gulp of water, and leaned back against the parapet of the machine-gun nest. Dix laughed near at hand, but kept his eyes on the distant shapes of the drift-ships patrolling beyond the Ile's perimeter.

"All right, Johnny," Stirling said patiently. "I keep on underestimating you; so I'm not going to point out the impossibility of fighting Hodder and Raddall. You must know that already. Just tell me what terms you can hope for."

"Hope for, big brother? I'm not *hoping* for anything. I told you, I'm laying down the terms." Johnny kept watching the eastern horizon as he spoke; and, following his gaze, Stirling saw the yellow outline of a robot approaching at top speed. It was too far away for him to see who was riding it.

"But think ahead, Johnny. You surely can't . . ."

"For Christ's sake!" Johnny flowed upright and turned his back on Stirling. "Do you ever get tired listening to yourself, Vic? You make such a profession out of sounding reasonable, and yet the things you say . . . Think ahead, you said. You want to talk about thinking ahead? You're good at that, are you?"

"Your 'rhetorical question' sign has just lit up, Johnny."

"Well, let's see how good you really are. Some of the people who came to the Ile to live brought guns with them, just in case they would be needed. Old man Latham brought his library. How about you, Vic? Supposing you had planned to stay on the Ile permanently, what would you have brought? What's the one thing you could have packed which would make it impossible for anybody in the whole world to order you back down?"

Stirling hesitated, unable to force his brain into action.

"I'll give you a few hints, Vic. The thing I brought weighs about five kilos; it's metal; and it's filled with a micro-powder called . . ." He waited, smiling.

"Herbicide," Stirling blurted out. "Paraquat dichloride-D!"

"Good boy," Johnny said with mock indulgence. "Isn't he a good boy, Dix?"

Stirling was too occupied with his own thoughts to note Dix's reaction. Johnny was unbalanced, of course; but it was possible to have too much equilibrium, to have a mind that was stable to the point of being static. Johnny's father, from whom he had inherited the ancient World-War-II flying boots, had been an antique aircraft enthusiast; and Stirling suddenly remembered him saying that the best fighting planes were slightly unstable.

And Johnny had piloted the slightly distorted, out-of-true craft of his mind with the lonely brilliance of an ace. The whole point about Heaven was that, in the eyes of the average American, *the soil was sacred*. That was the primitive psychology underlying the nation's acceptance of the fantastic cost of the air-borne islands in spite of their relatively insignificant output. They represented the cherished fecundity without which no organism can have a stake in the future, and to threaten even one of them with sterility was to wield a dark power against which little could stand. One herbicidal bomb exploded inside the Ile's shell field would render it meaningless, valueless, infertile.

There was a noise at the hatch, and Theodore's head appeared in the opening. "The set's working again, Jaycee, and somebody wants to talk to you and your brother."

"Who is it?"

"I'm not sure. I told you, I'm out of touch; but it looks like Administrator Raddall."

Johnny rocked back and forwards gently, eyes closed, smiling peacefully. "Tell Administrator Raddall I'll be happy to discuss my terms with him – after I've finished eating."

## Chapter Fourteen

It was not until the FTA withdrawal from the Ile was almost complete that Stirling could accept the idea of being free to take the big drop anytime he felt like it.

Among the miscellaneous supplies the villagers had found when they took the power station was a pair of powerful binoculars with a floating optical system designed to damp out tremors from the observer's hands. Stirling commandeered the glasses for his own use and spent several hours on the station's roof watching the evacuation of the FTA headquarters. The foreshortened perspectives of the binoculars showed the work going under a sky which was almost solid with the dark shapes of military drift-ships and the flitting bubbles of television camera teams. As the activity slowly died away, Stirling tried to muster the elation he should have felt at finally being free, but something was getting in the way.

Administrator Raddall had been surprisingly easy to negotiate with, possibly because of an instinctive appreciation of Johnny's methods; but Stirling suspected that a politician of his stature was not going to be beaten so easily. This feeling had been strengthened, rather than allayed, by Raddall's immediate use of the Special Powers Act of 1996 to order the FTA off the Ile, and his vague hints at the possibility of making the eastern end into a sort of reservation for the villagers. The discussion had taken place over an ultra-secure, tunnel-screened beam. Raddall's only stipulations had been that the villagers were to remain as inconspicuous as possible and the existence of the herbicidal bomb was to be kept a secret. Stirling could appreciate Raddall's desire to appear as a humanitarian rather than a statesman who had been outsmarted by a drifter; but was that a good enough reason for concealing the one factor which could justify his action in the eyes of the electorate? Or was he afraid the public would not hold still for blackmail? If Raddall was forced to act against the villagers, the resultant sterilisation of the Ile would represent an ugly blot on his career.

My trouble, Stirling thought irritably is that it's six months since I've killed a bottle of whisky. He set the binoculars down and lowered himself through the hatch. Johnny was lounging at the door, looking out across the darkening furrows, while Dix, Theodore and the others gathered up all the portable supplies left by the FTA garrison. They were chuckling as they worked, still filled with a kind of revolutionary fervour.

Johnny spoke to Stirling without looking around. "Are you coming back to the village with us, or staying here?"

"I guess you'll be celebrating tonight."

"We'll be celebrating tonight – the shields will be off the fires."

"One more night up here won't do me any harm," Stirling said. "I never tasted the local liquor."

"You could make the elevator before dark." Johnny kept staring straight ahead.

Melissa, Stirling thought, this is the night. There's going to be some celebration. The shields will be off the fires – right off.

"There's no hurry," he said carefully. "I haven't said my good-byes."

"Victor." Johnny turned, and Stirling saw he was speaking through the prosthetic without moving his lips. "Your father was not my father. We're not brothers."

Ranged along a robot's beam, the raiding party rode east in darkness and then set off on the eight-kilometre walk from the Ile's centre line to the village. Several stars cruised directly overhead; and, along the length of the perimeter wall, luminous gases crept like huge insubstantial glowworms. Johnny walked slightly ahead, cradling the metal sphere of his bomb. As they neared the village the lights of unshielded fires clustered in the blackness ahead, and Stirling tried to imagine what the celebration would be like. The villagers had struck him as being too solitary, too accustomed to surveying the night from their individual spider holes, to get together for a jamboree.

But he was wrong.

One man had gone back earlier in the day with the news that Jaycee had bested Administrator Raddall and won for the villagers the right to live openly on the Ile. The fires were blazing high; and the villagers were sitting around in large, noisy groups, working through their stocks of colourless beer and wheat liquor. A mob greeted Johnny and the others as they reached the outskirts; hands slapped them on the backs; female bodies thudded against them with lusty enthusiasm – the women were giggling, pushing, breathing alcohol. Eddies of smoke carried sparks into the knots of dark figures, mingled with the smell of cooking, and gave the scene an atmosphere of dark carnival.

For the first time since his arrival on the Ile, Stirling found himself accepted without reservation. He ate hungrily and washed the food down with gulps of burning spirit, and was pleased to discover that six months of abstinence had not deprived him of the ability to enjoy the familiar malty warmth.

"There you are, big fella," Biquard said out of the darkness. Two other dim, smiling faces hovered behind him. "I've brung a couple of the girls to meet you. Carla and Jo. I ain't forgotten how you jumped me, or anything like that; but you went over the wall yesterday – and I couldn't. Okay?"

"Say, he *is* a big fella." One of the women leaned against Stirling. Her hair was rancid.

"Excuse me," Stirling said. "I think I left my wallet on the piano."

As he moved away quickly through the Hieronymus Bosch landscape, he tried to suppress a feeling of unreality and wondered if owl cameras were drifting above him in the night sky. At first he had some difficulty finding the Latham place, until a remembered configuration of storage tanks showed him where to turn. *I always think a good address is* so *important, don't you?* He was guided by a gleam of candlelight during the last few paces of the journey until he was standing in the doorway where he had met Judge Latham – seemingly in another life. Melissa's black-clad body was coiled like a whip on the low bed.

"Oh, it's you." She sat up. "You startled me."

"It's all right. I haven't brought my chloroform."

"I thought you were . . ."

"Johnny. He's moving in here tonight, is he?"

"It's expected. This is Johnny's day."

"What are you, anyway?" Stirling became angry. "A life-size kewpie doll? When do they hand you over?"

"Why did you come around here, Victor?"

Feeling self-conscious, Stirling went into the room. "Melissa, you don't seem to understand that all this isn't *real*. You could shuck it off anytime you wanted."

"Why did you come around here, Victor?"

"I'm leaving in the morning . . . I think your father intended that you should go too, if you wanted."

"I couldn't live down there. I can still remember."

Stirling sat down on the bed. "It isn't all that bad. Some people get work out on the reclamation projects. They *really* live in the open."

"Breathing dust and eating petroleum yeast!"

"All right, then. We could go south and perhaps I'd get a job on . . ." Stirling broke off, suddenly aware of what he was saying.

"Did you come around here to propose to me?" Melissa smiled easily, showing even, white teeth; but he noticed the suggestion of a tremor in her lower lip, and his heart began a slow, heavy pounding.

"I think so. It's beginning to look that way." He leaned forward to kiss her, but she turned her face aside. Her hair smelled like the night wind.

"Go away, Victor," she said urgently. "It's no good."

"You haven't given it a chance." He took her in his arms,

holding off the first kiss until he had gathered her right in against him, body to body, thigh to thigh. For one exultant, ringing moment he felt her relax into it; then her weightless body went rigid.

"Well, this is very pleasant," a grating parody of a voice said at the door. "Warming her up for me, are you, Victor?" Johnny stood in the doorway, still cradling the herbicidal bomb, the orbicular symbol and the reality of his power. He was stripped to the waist.

Stirling rolled away from Melissa and stood up. "I can't let you go through with this, Johnny. You can't play games with human beings."

"Speak for yourself." Johnny's eyes flicked towards the bed. "I can think of lots of games to play with human beings."

"You don't seem to understand . . ."

"I understand you too well, big brother. You want to moralise at me and take my woman at the same time. Get out of here, before I push you right through the east wall."

Stirling suddenly remembered his dream about being thrust through a door in the wall, meeting his father, and telling him about Johnny. His father's eyes had filled with accusation. *Why?*

"It might be better if we talked it over, Johnny. You don't seem to have the Council with you."

"I don't need them." Johnny set the bomb down and flexed his body muscles, with a movement curiously like a cobra spreading its hood before the strike. He advanced slowly across the room; and Stirling, full of a strange timidity which was foreign to his nature, watched him soberly. The whole concept of physical combat was repugnant to him; yet his quick temper, impatience, and thoughtless use of sarcasm had brought many fights to Stirling, often when he least expected them. Always, when the chips were down, he had handled himself with emotionless efficiency; and always he had won. But how was he to fight Johnny? Would he be able to punch? Would he be able to stop? He raised his arms tentatively, half-heartedly, remembering the look in his father's eyes.

"Johnny," he said. "This won't prove anything."

"No?"

Johnny closed with him and swung a blow which Stirling countered with his forearm. He was surprised at the ease with which he had been able to intercept the punch – until the pain arrowed up into his shoulder. Johnny might have been wearing steel gauntlets, and he had *intended* the blow to be blocked. He followed it with others in a steady, predictable rhythm, smiling frozenly as Stirling stopped the punches. It dawned on Stirling that Johnny was planning to beat his arms until they were useless – in a contemptuous display of force – and then move in closer. Stirling found himself still reluctant to strike back, and he began to feel afraid of his own weakness. He backed away until he was trapped in a corner, with slow hammer blows pressing him against the walls.

"Stop it!" Melissa ran from the bed and threw herself between them.

"Stay back." Johnny pushed her away. "This doesn't concern you."

"Doesn't it?" Melissa recovered her calmness. "I think it does. I don't like the implications, Johnny."

"Meaning what?"

"Meaning," Stirling said, "that you can't play games with human beings. I think Melissa feels entitled to decide her own future."

"That's right, Johnny." Melissa walked away from them, suddenly in command of the situation, and Stirling got a prescient feeling of dismay.

"Melissa, you don't make decisions this way. Not this way."

"What decision, Victor? You flatter yourself, you know that?"

Johnny peered from one to the other in the candlelight, then a slow smile spread over his face. "You've really been pitching in, haven't you, Victor? What have you two been saying to each other?"

"Nothing. Nothing except good-bye," Melissa said. She began to untie the belt knotted at her waist.

"It isn't necessary."

"Good-bye, Victor."

Stirling had walked only a few yards from the Latham hut when he decided he should make another attempt. He turned back in time to see the yellow glimmers fading as the candle was extinguished. Beyond the black outline of the hut, the Moon was scimitaring down on the Ile's western horizon; and Stirling saw the silhouette of an army drift-ship cut through it, a witch-shadow in a world where magic was long dead.

He pulled his jacket tighter and began walking towards the elevator head.

## Chapter Fifteen

Stirling rode down from Heaven in solitary splendour, sitting in the middle of a freight car, which had been sent up specially for him when the monitoring crews saw his appearance at the elevator head. As the car lost height he found himself having to adjust to seeing the dawn from *below* – the gun-metal mists of the Atlantic rose up on all sides like confining walls, and the oyster-coloured sky became remote. He ignored the vague sense of loss and concentrated on the very real pains in his ears – brought about by the increasing air pressure – until the car had docked on the island station. Holding his head in both hands and grimacing like an idiot in an attempt to ease the torment in his ears, Stirling stepped off the car to meet a group of men in the whites of the Food Technology Authority.

He was rushed downstairs into a windowless office suite and away from the prying cameras of the bubblecraft which were still flitting at the minimum legal distance from the Ile. During the following three hours he was interrogated by FTA executives; police officials; civil servants; two generals and an admiral; a panel of grey men he recognised as being members of the Media Council; and a number of tight-lipped individuals whose background remained professionally obscure. Through it all he stuck to the formula he had agreed upon with Administrator Raddall: he was a journalist who had gone to foolish extremes to get a story; he had no real idea how many people were living on the Ile or how long they had been there; and he had sworn to the Adminstrator himself that, in the interests of social stability, he would keep quiet about the whole affair. The only information he gave freely and in full was an account of how Duke Bennett had arranged his trip to the Ile and had tried to ensure that he would arrive there dead.

Someone in Raddall's office must have paved the way for him, Stirling decided, because at noon on the same day he was smuggled ashore on an FTA skimmer. Before leaving the station he had showered and had been provided with fresh clothes and facilities for removing his conquistador's beard. In spite of having spent most of the previous night stumbling through the length of the Ile in utter darkness, he felt relaxed and fit as he sat in the back of a closed truck that was taking him into downtown Newburyport.

"Where do you want to get out?" The security man who was travelling with him was unexpectedly polite and friendly. Stirling was momentarily surprised at the man's attitude; then he became preoccupied with the realisation that the basic facts of survival had not altered. He still had to earn money, eat, and provide shelter for himself – even though these considerations had not been so important on the Ile.

"Drop me at the *Record* office . . . I guess I better see if I still have a job there."

"You will . . . Don't worry." The security man smiled unctuously, and Stirling automatically opened a new data storage file in the back of his mind. He tentatively labelled it, *FTA – Isolated observations suggesting dirty work behind the scenes*. The file was a ridiculously thin one, even when – after a moment's hesitation – his mental librarian added an item about the uncanny speed of his release from the FTA island. The Authority had as much power as the Government in some spheres; and, regardless of Raddall's influence, they could have buried him out there in the shadow of Heaven.

"I wish I could be as certain of that as you seem to be." Stirling probed very gently and saw the security man's long face freeze into impassiveness. *Uh-huh*, the librarian said, *item number three?*

When the truck had reached the *Record*'s offices, the driver called back to Stirling through a sliding panel; and he opened the rear door and jumped out. The truck immediately moved away, caught up in the solid, creeping congestion of the fifth-level traffic arteries. Stirling went into the building, found a vacant elevator, and dropped himself to the floor occupied by the newspaper. By the time the elevator doors opened he was sweating gently, and his new shirt was developing the familiar stickiness under the collar which was something he had not experienced in a long time.

At the door to the main editorial office he paused for a moment, then went in as inconspicuously as possible. He ran into an almost palpable wall of warmth, smoke, and used air which made his lungs quail. The long office seemed to have shrunk to about half the size he remembered it. Walls clamped in on an incredible montage of desks, screens, columns, service cables, and an impossible number of people who were working, talking, crouching over machines, smoking, and threading their way through narrow aisles with eel-like speed. Stirling felt his breathing lapse into a ragged, uneasy rhythm.

"Say! There's big Vic!"

A group of reporters surrounded him within seconds, some of them climbing over desks to get closer. He shook as many hands as possible and exchanged greetings with familiar faces to which he had a disquieting amount of difficulty in attaching names. The voices seemed to wrap him in a stifling blanket of sound.

"What was it like up there?"

"How did you lose so much weight? Didn't they feed you up there?"

"Tell us about the gun battles, Vic."

"Any women up there?"

"How much would it cost me to get a tan like that?"

"Did you bring any . . . ?"

In the middle of the confusion, a woman thrust a note into Stirling's hand. He opened it and read:

"Pl. see me when you've finished – S. McL."

Christ, Stirling thought in something approaching panic, McLeod is still sitting at his desk and sending notes to reporters who are all of five paces away. The walls seemed to

132

move in closer for an instant. He struggled free of the mob and worked his way across to the news desk. McLeod set down his plastic cup of synthejuice and stood up to shake hands.

"Welcome back, Victor." He smiled painfully. "It's good to see you again, Victor. Don't worry about your contract – the company is overlooking the irregularities; so you're still employed and have six months back salary to collect when you're ready for it."

Stirling prevented his jaw from dropping. "I didn't expect this, Sam."

"Think nothing of it."

"But after the way I walked out . . ."

"The company is taking heed of the special circumstances, what with your brother being missing, and all that. It must have been pretty tough for you. And besides" – McLeod toyed with his cup – "we can't afford to lose good reporters."

Stirling almost burst out laughing. McLeod had not been able to look him in the eyes and come out with that one, not after four years of private warfare between them.

"Well, thanks a lot, Sam. I had no idea the paper thought so much of me." Stirling allowed the faintest note of insincerity to creep into his voice and McLeod, a seasoned verbal skirmisher, looked at him thoughtfully from yellowed eyes.

"There is only *one* thing, Victor. Obviously you'll not be ready to start work right away, but Mr Selig left word he would like to see you for a few minutes at the earliest opportunity. Could you go down to his office now?"

Stirling nodded non-committally. As news editor McLeod was responsible to the *Record*'s editor, who in turn was answerable to the editor-in-chief of the company group of papers. Above him again was the general manager of the proprietary corporation, and then one reached Mr Selig, a man very few of the reporters had ever even seen. The librarian in the back of Stirling's mind opened up his brand new file and stood waiting.

"Well, Vic. You've been in the news lately."

133

"Yes. I'm doing my best to get back out of it again though."
Stirling leaned back in his chair and watched Leon Selig across
an expanse of cluttered desk. He was a thick, round man with
an incongruously tiny hooked nose which reminded Stirling of
a budgerigar's beak.

"Yeah, but the point is, you *got* into it by yourself. I like
that, Vic. It shows you've got initiative and imagination, two
qualities that are pretty scarce in the *Record* these days. I've
got some ideas for reorganising things upstairs, and I'll be
keeping an eye on you, my boy. This is between us, of course –
in the meantime, anyway."

"Thank you, Mr Selig." Stirling put a carefully calculated
amount of gratitude into his voice and wondered exactly what
he was being set up for. Selig appeared not to hear. He spent a
full minute tidying paperwork on his desk, while Stirling
concentrated on forcing his lungs to accept the machine-
cleaned, lifeless air. Selig's office – although palatial for one
man by Compression standards – was much more claustrophobic than the editorial room. He decided he would be able to
sit in it for a maximum of five minutes, perhaps less, if nothing
interesting happened soon.

"Now, Vic," Selig's voice was warmly confidential. "As you
know, I never interfere in matters of editorial policy, but
we're dealing with exceptional circumstances here. So, what I
would like you to do if you don't mind, is to outline for me the
kind of story you're planning to write about your experience."

"I'm not planning to write anything," Stirling said bluntly.
"I wasn't on an assignment. I went up there for personal
reasons."

"That's how a good story is written, Vic. When the reporter
isn't just an impartial observer, but is personally involved, we
get a good story, something that's worth reading. Now, look.
Your salary for the whole six months is being paid into your
account today, and I'm going to offer you a special rate for a
series of feature stories about those people up there. A dollar
a word. Write it to any length you like, at a dollar a word. How
does that sound?"

"It sounds great, Mr Selig, but I can't do the story."

Selig began tidying his desk for the second time around. "I understand that Lester Raddall talked to you up there?"

"Yes, but I'm not writing about that either."

"He can't touch you, Vic. We can all see his point of view, of course. He fluffed the whole business, by knuckling in to those bums, and now he wants the whole thing buried. It's understandable he should want it forgotten; and I admire the stand you're making, Vic. But don't get your loyalties misplaced.

"Your duty is to the people of this country, not to any individual or group."

"That's the way I feel about it," Stirling said. "And that's why I'm not going to write this story. I guess I'd better clean out my desk and start looking for another job."

Selig gave a booming laugh. "How little you know me, Vic. If, in your judgement, a story should not be printed, would no amount of money make you change your mind?"

"No." I don't sound like myself, Stirling thought. Am I going to be subject to rushes of idealism to the head? If so, I'd *better* look for another job.

"That's it, then. Integrity is too scarce a commodity in employees for me to try subverting it. I want you to know that the impressions I've formed in this private little talk will improve your promotion prospects, Vic.

"No, I don't want you to clear out your desk." Selig laughed again.

Stirling moved uneasily in his chair as he tried to loosen the bonds of perspiration gripping his clothes. "If there's nothing else . . ."

"Don't rush away . . . I've ordered some coffee." Selig pressed a button. "Let me confess something to you, Vic. I expect you're wondering why I had you down here in person, instead of handling this matter through the usual channels?"

"Well, I . . ."

"Of course, you were. You're not dumb. The truth is I wanted to talk to somebody who had been up there in person.

I'm not claustrophobic; don't get that idea; but those islands up there in the sky have always fascinated me, Vic.

"Tell me, what was it *really* like?"

Stirling hesitated, then gave a general description of the upper surface of International Land Extension, US 23, in which he was careful to put very little more than would be found in a good reference work. A grey-haired woman with cylindrical shins brought in the coffee; and, while they were drinking it, Selig asked a number of questions about how the villagers lived. He seemed naively disappointed to hear they had not developed a separate tribal culture complete with initiation ceremonies and fertility rites.

"I'm afraid they were a pretty uninteresting bunch," Stirling said as he stood up to drain the last of his coffee.

"They sound that way," Selig twinkled. "I guess I've always been too much of a romantic anyway."

When Stirling finally broke free of the *Record* office he went for a cold drink, but the bar's dark and airless confines made him feel as though he had been sewn up in black velvet. The beer tasted of chemicals, and he kept imagining the intertwining of tanned limbs – Melissa's and Johnny's. He decided it was time to go and see his mother.

On the way out of the bar he noticed a newspaper vendor at the door; then he remembered the world had been getting along without him for six months, and he had no idea what had been happening. He put a coin into the machine and waited while it printed the hourly edition. The pre-rush-hour lull was prevailing outside. He got a cab without any difficulty and settled down to read the paper during the trip. It was a single sheet and – being an electronic throwback to the *corantos* of the seventeenth century – carried a temporally narrow slice of the world's affairs.

It was the day of the full moon; and, as usual, there was a snide story about the billions of frustrated Chinese males who would be denied normal relations with their wives for the next four days, on pain of having their names displayed on wall posters as betrayers of the gloriously regulated and synchronised womanhood of China. There was news of the failure of TWEAK, the desperation project in which a multimillionaire had spent his whole fortune in launching a ship, which was all power plant and no payload, simply to find out, once and for all, if Einstein had been right and the stars really were unattainable. Crime and sports news filled out the bulk of the edition, and Stirling was throwing the sheet aside when his eyes picked out a familiar name, Mason Third.

The story contained no mention of the Receders. It simply stated that Senator Mason Third had announced he would ignore the Administrator's ban on his public rallies and speak in Boston that night on the Land Extension scandal. Stirling was astounded both by the use of the title "Senator" and the generally respectful tone of the copy. A lot must have happened in six months. He settled back thoughtfully in his seat and waited for the taxi to carry him home.

Mary Considine was intent on building a bouquet of artificial ferns when he opened the door and walked into the cramped apartment. She looked up and studied him for a moment with baffled eyes.

"Kill the fatted planktonburger," Stirling said finally. "I've come back."

"Are you going to stay here?"

"Yes, if you can fit me in."

His mother nodded casually, but he saw a furtive gleam of satisfaction in her eyes; and he wondered – for perhaps the thousandth time – what refinements of Twenty-first Century living had forced her withdrawal. Could it have been simply the sheer monotony of thirty-five years in a fam-apt? There was no way to find out, because her shell permitted no emotional communication in either direction. Mrs Considine uttered words when they were absolutely necessary, but she never talked. Moving with heavy patience through furniture which nudged her at every step, she pulled her sleeves down over her mottled, red forearms and began to prepare his bed. This, Stirling thought, is what I offered Melissa.

He spent the rest of the day at the television set, switching from channel to channel, trying to re-orientate himself in the world's affairs. The first thing he was able to confirm was that Mason Third really was a senator for Popmod 162, an area roughly corresponding to the seaboard of the old Georgia. Even under the streamlined electoral system introduced at the beginning of the century, Third had travelled far and fast – an indication that he had been preparing the ground carefully in advance. His ticket, from the tantalising references Stirling caught, seemed to be a dressed-up version of the Receders' anti-everything attitude. But the fact that a man could succeed in politics by being *against* the Food Technology Authority, the Iles programme, enforced population control – and apparently *for* nothing – carried alarming sociological implications for anybody who wanted to think about them. Stirling had no desire to think about anything at all, but it was necessary to numb his mind with information to prevent him noticing the slow inward creep of walls.

Another thing which immediately became apparent was that the FTA political machine had gone into action against the Government because of its dismissal from the Ile. Loaded connotations in straight newscasts, wisecracks by disc jockeys, heavily weighted magazine programmes, all hammered home the point that Administrator Raddall had acted against the FTA, yet had given a bunch of squatters unlimited freedom to trample down the nation's food under their unwashed feet. The propaganda was good and it was effective.

Late in the evening, Stirling tired of watching the FTA puppets dance on the ends of their all too visible strings. He tried to read and then to interest his mother in talking, but in the end decided to go out in search of air. At the bottom street level he stood on the sidewalk for several seconds, labouring desperately for breath, before he walked aimlessly towards the city centre. Sometime later he began to notice people staring.

Stirling had covered several more blocks, consciously watching out for the signs of recognition in strangers' eyes, before he saw his own face looking out from the billboard screen of a

*Record* news vendor. Beside it, the *Special Edition* sign was winking with its ruby light. Stirling had to join a short queue before he was able to drop in a coin for his own copy. The heading was:

## HOBOES IN HEAVEN – THE FULL STORY

Underneath it, a lengthy subheading said: "On Ile 23 a group of men who have no respect for society live high and wide off the nation's food supplies and thumb their noses at the American people. Victor Stirling, a *Record* reporter, was there! Here at last is the full story of the drop-out society – the men who made suckers of YOU!"

Accompanying the story was a three-column, head-and-shoulders picture of Stirling from the *Record*'s stock files, and another showing him being rushed away from the elevator car by the FTA men. The caption read, "After his six months' imprisonment on Ile 23, *Record* reporter, Victor Stirling, is helped from the elevator by the FTA officers who brought him down to safety." In the photograph Stirling was stumbling and holding his head, but there was no way of knowing this was a result of earache – a fact which had lent itself to the production of one of the most heavily loaded pieces of copy he had seen in a long time. He *had* been a prisoner on the Ile, but anybody reading the paper would get the idea he had been rescued by the FTA.

Stirling bulled his way through the tide of people to a backwater in the entrance of a store and scanned the main story. It was written in a luridly factual style for the most part, and the phrase "this reporter" occurred in passages expressing opinions. Nowhere was it actually stated that Stirling had written the story; yet, as far as the man in the street was concerned, this was an eyewitness account of life on the Ile. Stirling went through it, picking out echoes of descriptions he had given Selig earlier in the day. When he came to a paragraph telling how the villagers kept warm by burning tons of yellow grain, he screwed the paper up in a ball and began looking for a telephone. In the booth, he keyed the *Record*'s editorial number and got through to the nightman.

"Is McLeod there?" Stirling demanded.

"Not tonight. Who wants him?"

"When will he be back?"

"Eight-thirty in the morning. Who wants to know?"

Stirling dropped the receiver and walked back the way he had come. The reckoning with McLeod – and Selig, if he could be reached – would have to wait till morning. He forced himself to admit that the nightlong cooling off period was a good idea, because in his present mood he would have been capable of using one man as a club with which to beat the other to death. When he finally lay down in the coffin-like bedroom, he had to wait a long time before sleep came drifting down like black snow.

In the morning, while he was eating breakfast, came the news that Administrator Raddall had ordered complete evacuation of Ile 23.

## Chapter Sixteen

No shots were fired until the second day.

In view of the fact that the group on the Ile had either destroyed or merely quit using the communications set, Administrator Raddall's orders were transmitted to them by two United Air Force machines which flew the length of the eastern margin dropping leaflets. The instructions were that they were to assemble in an orderly formation and walk along the southern edge of the Ile, keep clear of the power station, and make their way to the elevator head where they would be shipped down to the island. A time limit of twenty-four hours had been set for the move to begin; and when it was ignored two more UAF machines – strike/reconnaissance craft this time – howled along the margin on another leaflet raid.

On their second pass, the amethyst needle of a rad-rifle flicked up from the village and separated the starboard wingtip of the lead aircraft from the rest of its airframe. The plane, with no height in which to manoeuvre, followed its fatal asymmetry into a banking dive, which intersected the level of the soil beds about a mile west of the margin. Its wing and empennage were wiped off as the heavy fuselage tore through the Ile's structure and fell, tumbling end over end, into the receptive waters of the Atlantic. The pilot died somewhere between Heaven and Earth.

In the second aircraft was an impulsive young man who, only an hour earlier, had been playing cards with his dead companion. He stood his aircraft on its tail; pulled it back across the hard blue sky in an immense, sun-glinting loop; and, during the vertical dive, unleashed a swarm of external stores at the spot where he imagined the village to be. As it happened, his guess was fairly accurate; and the only thing which saved the villagers from annihilation was the fact that the bombs were fitted with dibber fuses intended to let them penetrate at least ten feet into concrete before they exploded. The salvo splatted right through the Ile in a tight formation and layered the sky with black blossoms a few hundred metres further down. By that time the second pilot had calmed down sufficiently to listen to the orders being screamed at him, and he rolled away towards his mother carrier.

The long ribbons of winter wheat were still undulating gently as the Ile's structure absorbed the impact of the punch delivered by the first aircraft.

Stirling heard the news with a bleak sense of dismay. He guessed the rad-rifle marksman who triggered off the violence had been Dix; but he could not be sure. Johnny had travelled far enough along his own lonely road to be capable of such an action by himself. In any case, events had been channelled into a new and deadly direction, one in which the innocent were bound to suffer with the guilty. The innocent were personified in his mind as a dark whiplash of a woman with black hair which smelled like the night wind.

Stirling did not go into the *Record*'s office for his showdown with Selig and McLeod. It was, he realised, far too late. He spent the day at his mother's television set, leaving it only to brew strong coffee between newscasts – each long-focus shot of the Ile increasing his feeling of suffocation and helplessness. Stirling was vaguely aware that his own life had, at some point, been diverted into a strange new direction. Six months on the Ile had effectively deconditioned him as regards life in the Compression; yet there was nowhere else to go. Mankind, in one way or another, had used up all the living space allotted to it on its home planet; and the Solar System as a whole was not a residential neighbourhood.

In the afternoon came the news that a platoon of anti-grav troopers had tried a sneak raid on the Ile's power station. The garrison of villagers in the station had machine-gunned six of

142

them before their feet touched the soil, and the others had crawled most of the way back to the elevator head. Army spokesmen were quick to point out that it was impossible to use normal tactics against the squatters because of the risk of damaging the power plant and bringing the Ile down into the sea. This news inflamed public opinion to the point where crowds began to gather outside Government Mile in Boston. Another report said that the controversial senator, Mason Third, had flown north, ostensibly on private business, but was expected to organise demonstrations outside the monolithic administrative centre.

Flash point was finally reached when a bubblecraft rented by an English news agency got through the drift-ships and flitted across the Ile's eastern wall. It crashed a few seconds later, possibly through inexpert piloting; but as far as the man in the street was concerned, the squatters had begun murdering civilians. Raddall had no choice other than to give the army chiefs free rein to clear the Ile in any way they could.

When it was announced that strike aircraft had begun patrolling the margin and hosing lead at anything which moved, Stirling went to the phone. He spent an hour trying to reach Raddall; he grimly penetrated secretarial screens until, at the highest level, he was told bluntly that the Administrator would not speak to him.

"For Christ's sake!" Stirling shouted. "There are women and children up there. Raddall has to work this thing out some other way."

"Mr Stirling," the impersonal voice said. "You, of all people, should know that this situation was forced on the Administrator."

"I didn't write that story," Stirling protested.

"Does it matter? Surely this affair hinges not on the story's authorship, but on its readership. In any case, Mr Stirling, press publicity was only a very minor contributory factor in the Administrator's decision. My sincere advice to you is not to overestimate your responsibility."

Stirling drew an unsteady breath. "Take your sincere advice and . . ." The phone clicked and went dead.

He set it down and tried to relax; but, for the first time in his life, he was *involved*. Things had been very much more comfortable on the sidelines where one stared down at the marble faces of John and Jane Doe and made detached philosophical comments. But he had stepped into a game in which children wept in the heavy silence which follows machine-gun fire and men walked ropes above piled-up thunderheads. And he had breathed the night wind in black hair . . .

"Mother," Stirling said presently, "I have to borrow some money from you. I'm flying to Boston."

Mason Third was about fifty years old, with twinkly-eyed good looks, greying hair and the upright carriage of a vain man who is below medium height. He stood in the centre of his hotel room and read Stirling's note for the second time.

"What makes you think I can help you, Victor?" He spoke crisply, with an almost English accent, and Stirling momentarily saw him in a World War I officer's uniform, with direct eyes, neat moustache, Sam Browne belt. The physical presence of Mason Third had not matched Stirling's preconceived picture in any respect, except that an entry in his morgue file had connected him with a divorce scandal. This carefully dressed man, who barely came to Stirling's shoulder, was the archetype of all lady-killers.

"I know you can help me," Stirling said, sensing that a blunt approach would work best. "But what's more important from your point of view, is that I can help you even more."

Third glanced at his watch. "I don't quite see that."

"Senator, let's not beat about the bush. People are dying on Ile 23, and we both have good reasons for keeping them alive. My reasons are personal; yours are political. Right now Raddall has the voters behind him; but tempers are going to die down eventually and somebody's going to count the cost in human lives and state-owned property.

144

"Did you know my brother has a herbicidal bomb up there?"

"No." Third's eyes became watchful.

"He has . . . And he'll use it. Raddall is going to be the first Administrator to throw away hundreds of square kilometres of agricultural land almost on the eve of an election. That's the negative side. The positive side is that you could become the senator who *saved* that amount of agricultural land almost on the eve of an election . . ."

"Never try to become a politician, Victor," Third interrupted. "Broadswords and flick knives are incompatible weapons."

"If you can get me back onto the Ile," Stirling said doggedly, "I can get control of that bomb, and I can get those people up there to agree to come down peacefully."

"You're certain of that?"

"Yes."

Two hours later, as the elevator car carried him up into the windy darkness, Stirling looked back at the trembling lights of civilisation and pondered the meaning of that last affirmative. In retrospective analysis, it did not mean he was certain he could overcome Johnny, get control of the bomb, and win the villagers on to his side. All it meant was he was prepared to die in the attempt; but – Stirling looked up at the black trapezium of Heaven with something approaching reconciliation – he had just discovered that one brand of certainty was as good as another.

## Chapter Seventeen

Feeling grateful that somebody had been thoughtful enough to deactivate the robotic scarecrows, Stirling picked his way across the ice-covered transit area.

He hesitated at the edge of the raised platform and pondered a leap down into the crawling darkness which – for all the reassurance he got from his eyes – might represent a hole cut in the Ile's floor. Borges had fallen silently to an unpleasant death, Stirling thought. Air resistance prevents a man's body from reaching any higher speed than 200 kilometres an hour, which meant Borges would have had a full minute and a half to think things over on the way down.

The silhouette of a partially completed building further along the platform reminded Stirling that the FTA team must have provided some means of getting down to the soil bed level. He walked along the tracks, found a ramp, and walked down it. The intense darkness was accentuated by radial sprays of light on the horizon far ahead, where government aircraft had ringed the power station with perma-flares. Stirling was certain Johnny was not one of the garrison; and he did not want to get close to the station anyway, in case somebody opened up on him with a rifle. He kept moving south for the better part of an hour, jumping the sunken tracks which separated each fertile strip before turning east in the direction of the village. Once his eyes had adjusted to seeing by starlight, he found it relatively easy to keep in the centre of a strip. He had been striding over the crisply furrowed soil for some time before realising his chest no longer felt constricted, that his lungs were satisfying themselves easily and gratefully on the glacier-fresh night air.

*Johnny was right about me, he thought. More right than I was about him.*

By taking bearings from the garishly illuminated power station, Stirling estimated he had covered about twelve kilometres when the radio in his pocket began to bleep. He took it out and spoke his name into the grill.

"Victor," a crisp voice said, "this is Mason Third. I've just had clearance from Raddall. He isn't happy, but the Air Force is going to hold off until noon tomorrow – to*day*, that is. You'll need to have everything going your way by that time."

"Don't worry." Stirling dropped the radio into his pocket and began to walk faster, looking around him for the familiar hulk of an agricultural robot. The villagers had too much in common with frontiersmen for him to try sneaking up on them. The only way to enter the village in safety would be on the back of a yellow dinosaur.

An hour later he found one of the big machines quietly at work turning over the black soil, unhindered and unperturbed by the darkness that sifted away to the horizons. Stirling climbed up on the moisture-beaded flanks, crossed the beam, and positioned himself on the flat upper surface of the faintly thrumming turret. When dawn began to overpaint the dimmer stars he stripped the cover from the alarm relay panel. It came away easily in his hands and was evidence that this particular robot had been ridden in the not too distant past. He closed the relay designating the eastern end of the strip; the turret pulled its spider legs clear of the soil; and the steel mammoth obediently moved off with gathering speed. Stirling kept his face turned into the wind and sucked it in greedily while he had the chance.

The robot took ten minutes to reach the edge of the village. As soon as it had rolled to a halt, Stirling leaped onto the soil bed and from there down into the margin. Knowing his arrival would have been watched by dozens of eyes, he walked casually towards the centre of the village and waited for someone to make contact. He did not have long to wait. A man and woman ran towards him from the shade of a grass-blurred tank, the woman carrying a layered bundle which must have been a baby. Her face was voodoo-patterned with tear streaks.

"Can you help us?" Her voice was brittle with fear. "Can you get us out of here? My baby . . ."

The man did not speak; but his eyes scanned Stirling's face, and he kept touching the woman's shoulder uncertainly, almost apologetically.

"Everybody can leave," Stirling said. "The raids have been suspended till noon to give you a chance to get clear of the village. Spread the word around. Everybody is free to go."

The man hesitated.

"What are you waiting for? I tell you it's all over."

"Jaycee says nobody is to leave." The man glanced guiltily at the woman beside him. "He's sitting on a tank down at the south end. He has that rad-rifle up there with him – and he says nobody is to leave."

Stirling felt something heave icily in his stomach. "I'll fix it with Jaycee. Just start spreading the word around."

He walked on towards the south end, noting the effects of the air raids. The grass underfoot was matted and soggy in places where storage tanks had been ripped open by cannon fire and had spilled their contents, which was sometimes water, sometimes evil-smelling liquids. In several places he saw ragged three-foot holes in the decking, through which it was possible to glimpse sunlit oceans seemingly frozen in their westward march by sheer distance. Several times he saw brown faces watching him from the lee of heavier structural members. Each time, he waved confidently and shouted to them to get ready to leave; but they seemed afraid to move – and he had an idea they were not worrying about aircraft. He wondered if Johnny had burned anybody with the big rifle, just to show them that the king was not prepared to let his subjects walk out on him. Stirling hoped it had not come to that. Somehow, someday it could all be worked out and made right again – provided Johnny had not taken human life.

148

At the indistinct line which only a native could recognise as marking the southern end of the village, Stirling halted and looked around. Some of the tracks in the area were twisted into the air like sculpted lines of agony; and the bomb holes were giving off a low moaning sound as air bled through them from the higher pressure zone inside the Ile's shell field. Stirling was reminded of photographs taken in European cities at the end of World War II. He was cupping his hands around his mouth to call Johnny's name when he saw Melissa. She was slumped tiredly against the patchwork wall of a large hut. Her face was whiter than he had ever seen it, and her hands were streaked with red. It dawned coldly on him that she had been watching his approach for some time, but had not bothered to signal her presence.

"Melissa!" He ran towards her. "Are you all right?"

"I'm alive," she said dully. "Why have they stopped? Where are the planes?" Her eyes were unfocused, vacant with shock and exhaustion.

"There won't be any more planes. All we have to do is get out of here in a hurry."

"Get out?" Melissa raised one hand to her forehead, and he saw it was covered with blood. "Get out? I can't leave." There was a movement in the hut behind her, and his eyes suddenly picked out the horizontal figures of men, or women, lying in the dimness. Somebody began to groan; the sound came as regularly as breathing. He went to the door, looked in, and turned away quickly.

"Don't go in there again, Melissa," he said quietly. He took her arm and led her away from the hut. "You aren't even entitled to accept that sort of responsibility. I'll see that military medics are brought in as soon as possible."

She looked up at him, smiled uneasily, and became heavy in his arms. Stirling lifted Melissa and carried her limp body back to the last place where he had seen other villagers.

"Get out of here," he shouted, as he laid Melissa on the grass. "What are you waiting for?" There was no response, and he began to feel afraid that noon would come and find

149

them all frozen in the same tableau. "I tell you the raids have been stopped until noon. You can all leave."

"Give it up, Victor," a reedy voice said from above. "You haven't got the touch."

Stirling looked up and saw Johnny standing on the upper surface of a storage tank. He had spoken without moving his lips – the boyhood convention for menace – and the muscles around his mouth were slack and heavy. The bulky tubularity of the rad-rifle was cradled in his arms with its tripod still attached. Slanting across his bared chest was the strap of a pack containing a spherical object; and – Stirling felt a pang of fear – on his feet were the ancient, crinkled, leather flying boots left behind by his father. Suddenly Stirling saw his own father against that fabled background of misty dream-fields; the familiar-alien face taut with anger, his eyes accusing.

"Go away, Victor," Johnny squeaked. "You don't belong here."

*I'm older than you*, Stirling thought in a gust of inexplicable fury. *I was first! I BELONG!* He felt himself begin to run, heard his feet hammer on the thinly covered decking, and saw his limbs go hand-over-hand up the clustered feed pipes leading to the top of the tank. Halfway across the tank's upper surface he saw the look of hard speculation in Johnny's eyes, and his censor clamped down violently forcing him to slow to a walk. The understanding, which had been close at hand for a few seconds, receded, and left in its wake a sense of loss mingled with a vast relief.

"It's been agreed that the raids will be suspended until noon, Johnny." Stirling concentrated on keeping his voice under control. "That gives the people here plenty of time to get away."

Johnny shook his head. "You'll never understand. There are people who can't *live* down there. They don't want to leave."

"Some of them do, and the rest would probably go if you told them."

"That's what Raddall would like – to split us up. If he can

get the weaklings to leave of their own accord, he'll switch over to gas; and then it'll be all over."

"But it's all over right now. For God's sake, Johnny, be reasonable. Raddall has no choice other than to bring you down, one way or another. How long do you think *any* country could tolerate what amounts to a petty dictatorship within its own borders?"

Johnny smiled indulgently. "Within its own borders? You know, Victor, you have accidentally come close to the point of the whole operation. I do believe that if you were given a week or two to sit down and think about it, you would get there by yourself."

"This is . . ." Stirling began to speak impatiently, unthinkingly; then an idea was born. "You haven't the engineering know-how, Johnny." He spoke urgently.

"Not personally," Johnny said. "But the Council has it – and we're all one."

"But . . ." Stirling's mind was swamped with the new concept. "Even if you did master the negative-gravity units, and introduce a horizontal component, how fast would the Ile move? Five knots? Ten? No matter which way you go, they'll stay with you. It won't . . ."

He stopped speaking. Johnny was pointing straight up into the sky. Meaningfully.

# Chapter Eighteen

In a way, Stirling was almost grateful.

The idea was crazy, of course; but it was the kind of purposive craziness with which he could sympathise and almost understand – and it explained so much. Johnny's continual discussions with other Council members, the uneasy awe he seemed to inspire in so many of the villagers, his apparent disregard for consequences – all these became understandable in the light of Johnny's vision of the future. Stirling had no doubt the original idea had been his brother's. In it he could hear echoes of Johnny's own voice, the one he had had as a child, before a glass dagger ripped open his throat. The fair-haired, gap-toothed kid, who had leaned on the same window ledge as Stirling while they waited for a signal from Heaven, had been the author of this plan to turn the Ile into a 24-kilometre-long spaceship and fly it to . . . ?

"The Moon," Johnny said.

"There's no real need for us to put the Ile down anywhere; but the Moon will provide gravity and, somehow, it helps to have a *target* to act as a fixed frame of reference. The Moon. I always think a good address is so important, don't you?"

"Most good addresses have air and water laid on."

"We have all we need – all that's necessary is to make sure we don't lose it. This can be done by boosting the Ile's shell field to maximum impermeability. It won't be perfect, naturally; but it should retain air and moisture for twenty or thirty years . . . and that's enough to be getting along with."

"With those holes in the decking your air wouldn't last twenty or thirty minutes in space."

Johnny frowned momentarily. "You've got a point there,

but that's the sort of job the maintenance robots can handle. They aren't doing anything on it yet because the work we're doing in the power station has interrupted certain supplies. The hole where that aircraft went through is going to hold us back by a couple of days, though . . .

"You were right about Dix – I'll give you that. He was the one who chopped up the plane. I should have dumped him long ago."

"Where is he now?"

"I told you – I dumped him."

"Literally?"

"Yeah. Through one of the bomb holes. Poetic justice."

Stirling opened his mouth, but closed it again without speaking. Johnny could not have made a better choice than Dix for his first venture into death-dealing. His action could even do him some good with Raddall, but Stirling hated to think of any man going out that way.

"What do you say, big brother?"

"What do you expect me to say?"

"Well, you've always had plenty to say in the past."

"All right." Stirling looked past Johnny and saw that some instinct was bringing the villagers out of their spider holes to watch the confrontation. "How many of those people down there know about your plan? And how many of the ones that do know are in agreement?"

Johnny shrugged. "How many of the people down *there* want to eat pap all year round and live in coffins?"

"That's different. Nobody's gambling with their lives."

"Nobody's gambling *for* their lives, you mean. They haven't a chance. But the way I have things worked . . ."

"Johnny!" Stirling felt that to wait any longer would be dangerous in some unspecified way. "Raddall is holding off his planes till noon; and before that, I'm going to walk out of here and take everybody with me who wants to go."

"I can't permit that. Theo and the others in the power house need another five or six days. So, nobody goes back."

"I say different." Stirling looked squarely into Johnny's

153

eyes. For a few seconds there was absolute silence; then he saw that Johnny was twisting his body slightly, so that the muzzle of the rad-rifle – which had been pointing obliquely past him – was moving in an almost imperceptible arc into line with Stirling's stomach. He put his hand out with studied casualness and grasped the muzzle. Johnny smiled with one side of his mouth and began to apply pressure, using the full length of the weapon for leverage. In order to keep out of the line of fire, Stirling had to move sideways; and they began a slow, shuffling rotation. A ring of villagers had gathered to watch the deadly saraband take place on the high platform of the tank. As Stirling moved around under the relentless force of the rifle, he saw Johnny alternately outlined against a background of misty soil beds or the beaten pewter of the Atlantic visible over the eastern wall.

"Johnny," Stirling said desperately. "What are we doing?"

"Anybody who isn't for me is against me."

"'Jaycee' speaking again, Johnny?"

"I told you before – I don't like that stuff."

"But what can you do? You won't burn *me*."

For an answer, Johnny squeezed the trigger, and a blinding amethyst torch searched past Stirling's ribs. He let go of the stinging metal involuntarily, tried to grab it again, missed, and drove forward against Johnny's chest. Johnny grunted with surprise as the impact carried him backwards. They staggered across the tank, on the point of overbalancing; then Johnny's heels caught the upraised rim of the iris where the robots inserted their drinking tubes; the two men went down; and the rifle skidded away on the damp metal. As they scrambled to their feet, Stirling threw in his right and felt pain streak up his arm from a damaged fist. He had connected with the metal sphere of the bomb slung from Johnny's neck. Johnny seized the advantage and closed in with a flurry of practised, crushing blows. Stirling, who had never trained and who had always relied upon the sheer destructive power of the battering-ram that nature had given him for a right arm, fenced unsuccessfully with his left.

As he felt the solid, thudding blows rob him of the ability to move, he tried hitting back with his right, but the punches he landed harmed him more than Johnny. His hand seemed to be broken. He backed towards the fallen rifle and momentarily gave up any attempt to defend himself as he stooped to pick it up. Two crippling punches smacked into the small of his back, and he felt his knees begin to buckle. Johnny shouldered him contemptuously away from the rifle; and, as he toppled, Stirling clawed the air for support. His hands encountered the heavy sphere of the bomb, still in its pouch. He gripped the bomb hard, settled his heels against the metal underfoot, and swung Johnny away from the rifle. Johnny was lifted into the air before the strap of his pouch snapped. He came down on one foot right on the edge of the tank and skidded out into empty space.

Stirling set the bomb down and looked over the edge. Six metres below, Johnny was lying motionless in a patch of wiry grass, and his knees were drawn up to his chin like those of a small boy in an extravagant posture of sleep.

Cradling the rifle in his right arm, Stirling climbed down the feed pipes – noticing for the first time that pieces of plastic had been lashed to them to serve as a crude ladder. The villagers stood back silently as he ran around the braced legs of the tank to the spot where Johnny was lying. He turned him over gently. A huge bruise was domed across Johnny's forehead, and a single trident of blood ran from his mouth across one cheek.

"How is he?"

Stirling looked up and saw Melissa. "He'll live."

"Oh!"

Stirling had no time to work out whether the monosyllable signified relief or disappointment. Some of the villagers who had gathered around were staring at him with a kind of grinning uneasiness; they were obviously teetering on the brink of taking up the battle where Johnny had been forced to leave off. He wondered if their hesitation sprang from the ambivalence which had always been present in their attitude to his brother, or if they were showing a normal respect for the rad-rifle.

"Let's get one thing very clear," Stirling said steadily. "I've been back down on the ground, and you haven't. So, I know better than Jaycee or any of you what has been going on. And I can assure you the Administration is going to keep up the pressure till the Ile has been cleared. Anybody who wants to get out before the raids start again, should head for the southeast corner right now. The rest of you might as well jump through one of those bomb holes. It'll be quicker that way."

He finished speaking and stood staring into the encircling faces, none of which showed much sign of conviction. *You haven't the touch*, Johnny had said, and Stirling was beginning to understand what he had meant.

"Well, what are we waiting for?" It was the husband of the woman he had met on the way into the village. "Are we going to stay here and get shot to pieces? Me and Joanna's getting out while we got the chance."

His yelping voice had a raw edge of fear which broke the mental stasis of the group. Some of them began to drift away to the south, while others scurried towards their huts and spider holes to collect still valued possessions. Once the movement had begun, it accelerated until the villagers were almost in a panic to get away.

"What are we going to do about the wounded?" Melissa had regained much of her usual composure, but her eyes were taut with fear and strangely reminiscent of his mother's. He resisted an impulse to put an arm around her shoulders and tell her she would soon adjust to the Compression. There were lies, and there were lies – even for a young girl with an old woman's eyes.

"Leave them till the medics get here," he said. "We'll get clear as soon as possible. Can you stay on your feet?"

"I guess so."

"Then get somebody to call up two robots. That should be enough for the lot of us. How exactly do they do it, when there's no crop to damage?"

Melissa shrugged. "Something to do with water. I'll get it done." Her voice was faint and lifeless as she turned and walked away, leaning sideways once, mechanically, to pluck a long stem of grass. Stirling unwound a length of plastic rope from the ladder on the side of the nearby tank, and used it to tie Johnny's wrists and ankles.

There was no sound as the villagers rode west.

Stirling had tried to use the radio to let Mason Third know everything had gone according to plan; but its case was cracked and flattened, and there had been no response. Close to one end, he sat astride the beam of the big robot and kept his eye on the other machine following a short distance behind on the adjacent strip. Once or twice some villager further along the beam began to sing; but the idea failed to catch on, and the plaintive words trailed away behind, swirling out across the soil beds in flat invisible eddies. Melissa was on the other robot, but he found it hard to pick her out in the solid row of blackly ragged humanity perched along the beam. Beggars, refugees on horseback.

As far as Stirling could tell, the exodus had been joined by every member of the village community who was still breathing and able to walk. Almost directly below him, Johnny lay on the upper surface of the bogey. He was conscious; but his wrists and ankles were still bound, and extra loops of plastic prevented him from rolling over the edge. His eyes were unreadable black slits under the bruised mound of his forehead. Stirling found himself avoiding looking down. *Of course I'm my brother's keeper. Would you like to see his cage?*

He shifted his position on the beam and looked northwards to the distant outline of the power station. Theo and the other technicians Johnny had recruited were still in the station, but there was no way of telling if they had noticed the evacuation of the village taking place. Stirling decided to leave them to find out for themselves. He was turning away again when a cold, disquieting thought stirred in his mind. There had been something wrong about the appearance of the power station.

157

Shielding his eyes from the whipping breeze, Stirling stared at the rectangular block. Several seconds went by before he was able to accept the fact that its proportions had altered. The building was longer and lower in appearance, as though it had begun to sink into the ground – only there was no ground to receive it! As he watched, the sinking motion which had previously been imperceptible gradually accelerated, and the power station sank completely out of sight.

Stirling went rigid with shock and waited for the feeling of weightlessness which would signify that – deprived of its power source – the Ile was falling into the Atlantic. Nothing happened, except that the robot continued to thunder westwards, trembling and swaying slightly beneath him. He fought off the feeling of unreality for a few seconds. Then the top of the station reappeared on the horizon. The featureless block rose steadily until it was higher than he had ever seen it before, paused, and began to sink again.

Suddenly, Stirling knew what was happening. The Ile had begun to undulate like a gigantic blanket flapping in the wind.

Hoarse shouting from further along the beam announced that somebody else had become aware of what was happening. A woman joined in with a shrill scream as, for the first time, the movement of the huge structure made itself felt. The gentle sinking motion chilled Stirling's stomach and made him grip the beam with an instinctive, useless reaction.

"Look over there!" The man beside Stirling gripped his arm and pointed away, across the Ile, diagonally ahead of the robot.

A sharply defined ripple was sweeping across the soil beds. Fountains of dark earth, thrown up by the buckling of the underlying pans, feathered the air above the advancing crest, like an artillery barrage. It became obvious that they were going to intercept the ripple in a matter of seconds – and the robots were travelling at 80 kilometres an hour.

"Stop!" Stirling shouted, trying to make himself heard above the noise; but the villager lying on the underslung turret was already fumbling with the machine's alarm relays. The robot abruptly slowed down and was rumbling to a halt when the surface below it lifted savagely, erupted earth, and sickeningly fell away again. Sprays of dirt lashed the row of villagers, who were clinging precariously to the beam. Stirling was deafened by the awful sounds of cataclysm, the vast, shuddering groans of metal structures being overtaken by failure: tearing, grinding, crunching, ringing, snapping.

From his position at the end of the beam he saw the tracks far below him part momentarily – allowing daylight to spill *upwards*, reflected from the ocean five unthinkable kilometres down – then the tremor was past. As the robot returned to an even keel, and silence descended, Stirling looked up greyly, as though he was trying life on for size. The substructure of the Ile had been punished, but it had failed-safe – this time. He decided that Johnny's technical experts working in the power station had made a mistake or had taken a calculated risk. Either way, he did not want to be on the Ile when the next major adjustment to the power unit was attempted.

"Let's go," he shouted. "Let's get out of here."

The robot moved away again, crunching on dirt-strewn rails; and the second machine followed close behind it. They had almost reached full speed when Stirling realised Johnny was gone. He stood up for a moment and looked back the way they had come, but in all of Heaven's broad acres there was no sign of life.

"All right, Johnny," he whispered. "You and I are not brothers."

# Chapter Nineteen

There had been three mild tremors during the nightmare ride to
the Ile's western rim and the subsequent eight kilometres
march to the elevator head. Each time, Stirling had closed his
eyes to wait it out and, each time, had seen a familiar face, stern
and accusing. When we reach that elevator, he told himself, I'm
going down below with all the others. Nobody could expect me
to do anything else, not even my – another part of his mind had
sent up a frightened clamour, trying to obliterate the thought,
but Stirling had forced it through – not even my *father*. Comple-
tion of the thought brought a feeling of catharsis, of release; and
at the same time, the certain knowledge that he was caught in a
trap which had been sprung on him a thousand years earlier.

Now he was looking at Melissa across two sets of ice-
encrusted barriers: one on the elevator car, the other on the lip
of the docking bay. The wind made irregular moaning sounds in
the light-spewing gap between the two structures. Stirling
turned in the direction of the monitor cameras and waved both
arms. Red lights glowed suddenly on the corners of the freight
car, and caused the villagers inside it to glance around them
uneasily.

"Melissa," he called above the wind. "Don't worry. It's going
to work out."

She smiled wanly and nodded, making him aware of how
inane his words must have sounded. How could it work out?
Melissa's personality had already begun to crumple, and the
jaws of the Compression were scarcely beginning to close.
When the car dropped away, he kept his eyes on her face until
the cold, brilliant air blurred his vision; then he turned in the
direction of the power station.

\*

Stirling could have travelled faster by running down the centre of a strip; but the risk of being seen from the station would have been too great, and he kept at track level. His heavy rifle seemed to become more awkward with every kilometre he covered, but he jogged along the track bed determinedly by stiffening his ankles to prevent them turning on the uneven surfaces. The air seemed to have become colder and thinner, stinging his throat and lungs as he laboured to keep up the pace. There was no movement of aircraft near the power station, but dark specks disturbed the Ile's milky canopy far away to the southeast. He guessed the Air Force was lifting the wounded villagers to safety, and the load of his self-imposed responsibility eased slightly.

The act of moving quickly, without overbalancing or acquiring a broken leg, left little capacity to spare for thinking; but stray thoughts occasionally leaped into the forefront of his mind and hovered there, dancing, like targets supported on a spray of water. *Why am I doing this?* Where is Melissa right now? *What am I doing, anyway?* Where is Melissa right now? *Can my brother survive this?* Where is Melissa?

The second major ripple almost took Stirling unawares.

He was about three kilometres from the power station and sinking deeper into his maelstrom of repetitious thoughts, when the channel in which he was moving suddenly glinted with daylight far ahead, like the surface mirages on a sun-baked road. The patch of brilliance raced towards him like a pool of quicksilver speeding down an incline; then he realised it was being carried along a massive wave front. Daylight was spilling up between the soil beds as the structural distortions associated with the wave pulled them apart. Stirling looked blankly down at his feet. There was one on each track, and in a matter of seconds there was going to be nothing except thin air right where he was standing.

He hurled the rifle up onto the soil bed on his right and tried to vault up after it, but his foot slipped on the dewy metal. Instead of rolling easily into the green-gold wall of winter wheat, he scrabbled ineffectually at the edge of the huge pan and slid back down onto the tracks. The vast groaning sound he had heard once before caught up with him, and the rails beneath his body began to stir like live creatures. He leaped upwards just as the surface between the rails opened up into a broad highway of light and space. His hands caught two slim bundles of wheat stalks which promptly uprooted themselves and allowed him to slide backwards into the lethal fountain of brilliance. The edge of the pan raked across his wrists; he gripped it and hung on while hell's legions battled around him. He was lifted upwards so violently he was almost separated from his metal life line, and at the same time a fierce rush of air blasted downwards past him into the low pressure zone outside the Ile's shell field.

Stirling clung on, at the centre of the inhuman power contest, while the steel forests of the substructure shrieked in torment. As abruptly as it had arrived, the wave passed by on its journey to the rim; and the adjoining strips dropped back together again with a sound like two moons colliding. Stirling was driven down onto the tracks with a blow that paralysed his solar plexus and shut off his breath. He lay on his back between the rails. He was aware that a secondary ripple might part them at any second, but was completely unable to do anything about it. No breath, no movement, he thought with a sense of having been relieved of an irksome duty. It was not until the ability to gulp air had returned fully that he felt any compulsion to get to his feet and retrieve the rifle.

A low, whistling noise accompanied him as he moved off. He discovered that the previously invisible joint between the strips could now be seen as a hair-crack in the surface, and the Ile's air was escaping through it. The structure had withstood its punishment remarkably well, but it was nearing the limits of the redundancy which had been designed into it. Stirling put his head down and tried to move faster, anxious for the ground not to drop away beneath his feet.

The power station's single door, above the Ile's surface, was on the north side. Stirling began cutting diagonally across strips to approach it from the rear. He was checking the mechanism of the rad-rifle as he went. The air was notice-ably colder and thinner; and smoke from the guttering perma-flares was drifting low across the soil in insubstantial black ribbons and creating the atmosphere of a winter battle-field. He got into the station's shadow, activated the rifle, and slowly moved towards the entrance. It occurred to him that he had got there very easily – which was faintly surpris-ing, considering how careful Johnny had been about posting look-outs earlier. Ignoring the flickerings of unease, he stepped around the corner and saw the blunt nose of a machine gun projected from the central doorway. Noting the silvery bullet splashes on the metal, Stirling kept his back against the wall and moved towards the door until he could hear voices inside the building.

". . . last time, Jaycee, there's not enough *control*. Unless we take a month and go for a system with infinite resolution –and I mean *infinite* – we're going to rip this plant right out of the raft."

"We haven't got a month, and we don't need a month." Johnny's voice was shrill, rapid, like a speeded-up record-ing.

"Well, I don't see how it's going to work, that's all." The voice was both surly and dubious. Stirling recognised it as belonging to Theo.

"I'm not asking you to see anything. Just do what we agreed we could do."

"The original plan gave me a couple of months or more. You know, Jaycee, you'd fall too – just like the rest of us."

"Meaning what, Theo? Meaning what?" Johnny's voice was like glass shattering.

"Meaning, Mr Jesus Christ, that you really *can't* walk on water, or on air."

Don't say things like that, Stirling thought, don't ever . . . A man sobbed with pain, and the sound was follo-wed by a series of sickening, meaty thuds. Stirling put the muzzle of the rad-rifle through the doorway and looked inside. Theo was lying on the cable-strewn floor; Johnny was standing over him and staring reprovingly at his own fists. Four other villagers were looking on with carefully expressionless faces.

"Now what made me do that?" Johnny smiled sadly and was stooping to lift Theo when he saw Stirling. He shook his head disbelievingly. "Do *you* know what made me do that?"

"You had to do it, Johnny." Stirling stepped inside, past the unattended machine gun. "You couldn't overlook a case of *lèse-majesté*. Or was it blasphemy?"

"You shouldn't have come back, Victor."

"Let's not go through all that again," Stirling said with a weariness he really felt. He looked at the other men in the gloomy, stinking room. "You're all going down below, and you've a choice of two ways. Run for the elevator, or stay here and shake the Ile to bits. Which is it to be?"

One of the villagers, a red-haired man named Hewitt, stepped forward immediately. "All we needed was time. It would have worked, you know. We could have flown this thing anywhere."

"Perhaps," Stirling said. "Take Theo with you when you leave."

Hewitt shrugged, then nodded to the others; and they began to gather the unconscious man off the floor.

"You fools," Johnny squawked. "He's the one who robbed you of that time." In his anger he overloaded the prosthetic in his throat, and some of the words were almost lost in a querulous whine. "Our own city on the Moon. There's nothing to stop us."

Stirling ignored him and addressed himself to Hewitt. "The Ile has been evacuated, so you have no hostages. If you move it at all – especially if anyone gets the idea you would like to get it over a city – Raddall won't hesitate to vaporise the lot. As well as that, the Ile's leaking air at every joint . . ."

"Come on you guys," Hewitt interrupted. "What are we waiting for?" They raised Theo clear of the floor and carried him out.

The last man hesitated at the door. "Jaycee, I . . ."

Johnny silenced him with one shrill obscenity, turned his back, and swaggered further into the room.

"You too, Johnny," Stirling said curtly. "We're all going down together. You're the main reason I came back."

"I'll say." Johnny kept walking; and Stirling, following behind him, saw he was heading for the master circuit breakers, the ones from which he had burned the locks on his first day in the power station.

"Johnny!" Stirling spoke huskily. "Don't go near that panel."

"If you're going to burn me, you'd better do it now because I'm . . . *there!*"

Johnny leaped forward and laid his hands on the red-glowing handles. Stirling squeezed the trigger of the rifle, but nothing happened. For a second he thought the weapon had failed to function; then he realised the fault had been in his finger. It had refused to move. Johnny looked back over his shoulder, read Stirling's eyes, and smiled triumphantly.

"As you said, Victor – we're all going down together." He again spoke without moving his lips, and Stirling suddenly appreciated that the action had a peculiar relevance to the situation. They *were* boys again, and terrible things were about to be said between them. Things which, to the savage, boyish mind, could not be said without all the outward manifestations of menace and hatred. The speaking without moving lips; the grotesque imitation of a World War II Gestapo officer; the ritual ripping open of the fly, which placed the other boy at a shameful disadvantage; the threatening with fists or weapons; Johnny wearing his father's boots, the symbols of virility, of male aggression, of invading strength.

"I'll say I was the real reason you came back, big brother."

This has all happened before, Stirling thought, and he backed away in fear. *Are you going to do it?* His father's voice was real, accusing. *Or are you going to let me down again? You must realise . . .*

"I don't want to hear it," Stirling shouted, still backing away.

"But you *must*," Johnny said reasonably. "I can see you've blocked it all out again, Victor, and that's not good. It's important for you to know why you ran away from the fam-apt at the first opportunity, why you had to come here after me, why you had to take away everything I had, and why – even now – you couldn't burn me to save your life."

"I'm warning you, Johnny."

"But there's nothing for you to feel guilty about, Victor. You were only a kid when your father disappeared. You couldn't have been expected to defend your mother's bed; so there's no need for you to feel anything at all when you look at me. The only connection between us is that my father took your mother to bed and . . ."

Stirling threw the rifle aside and dived for Johnny's throat with clawing fingers; he caught the metal disc of the prosthetic and ripped it away from the flesh. *Try to say it now!* Johnny made a thick choking sound, and crimson bubbles appeared on the side of his throat. He thrust Stirling away with one hand, and with the other pulled all the circuit breakers. Stirling and his brother locked eyes for one frozen minute.

Then Heaven fell away beneath them.

The fall began slowly; the huge structure continued to support itself for a few seconds, until its output-smoothing reservoirs discharged the last of their stored energy into the power grid. Stirling turned and ran blindly from the power station; he found himself bounding across the surface in gigantic dream-leaps, making a nightmare escape where no escape was possible. His steps grew longer and longer as gravity appeared to vanish, and instinct told him he would part company with the soil beds forever unless he stopped moving. He arced headfirst into the uncaring wheat and held on, as if trying to steal some of its blithe immortality.

Full weightlessness arrived an instant later, and with it the now familiar sounds of Armageddon: groans so deep and vast that each separate vibration was a thunderclap in its own right; near-human shrieks; ear-splitting reports as structural members went beyond their limits of elasticity, and snapped clean, or were torn apart at their laser-welded seams. Some of the negative-gravity booster units patterned across the grid used their dregs of power more efficiently than others, thereby imposing even greater strains on the substructure; and the Ile broke up into immense flat sections. Stirling, looking up in fascinated horror, saw the ruler-straight horizons writhe and shiver themselves into misty fragments. The sky darkened above him as the segment to which he was clinging dipped one edge and slid in below others. Blurred backdrops of triangulated girders moved by in slow motion – rocking, spinning, receding – while the up-rushing wind roared and chanted in his ears.

Stirling screamed once, heard nothing, and found himself, incredibly, looking at the power station across a cloud-streaming gap. Although it was on a separate fragment, it appeared to remain fixed for a moment through a chance matching of velocities and directions. Johnny, his bare torso streaked with blood, appeared in the doorway. He gripped the doorframe with one hand and held something dark aloft with the other, waving it triumphantly in the air like a battle trophy. Then the power station canted ponderously and went into a slow rotation which carried it out of sight.

Stirling closed his eyes. Johnny had been holding his father's ancient flying boots.

Eons later he felt the return of gravity starting gradually, and increasing to a fierce pressure which drove him down into the matted roots. Stirling opened his eyes to a scene of aerial majesty. The flat segment, to which he was clinging, had side-slipped until it was almost clear of the mêlée; and it was now slicing upwards. Beyond its lower edge, kilometre-long fragments of the Ile descended towards the ocean in a lazy, spinning, countermarching, colliding swarm. Many of them trailed swirling black streamers of earth. Yellow motes, which were agricultural robots, plummeted vertically through the swarm, while military drift-ships hovered outside it against a brilliant background of sunlit ocean, monolithic clouds, and the seriate towers along the coast.

As Stirling watched, his own segment completed its upward sweep and curved into the chaos again like a fighter plane returning to a dogfight. The falling-leaf motion carried it deep into the swarm and miraculously back out again – once, twice, three times – before it reached the ocean. When the grazing impact came, Stirling cut an untidy furrow through the wheat strip for over a hundred metres – squandering a fortune in kinetic energy in the process – and then he was treading the icy waters of the North Atlantic in clear sunlight.

The shadow of Heaven had been lifted.

## Chapter Twenty

Sometimes, during the long night, Stirling would awaken with the knowledge that Melissa was not asleep. He would touch her forehead and find it as cold as dewed marble. On those occasions he always got up to brew coffee; and they would sit together in the darkness, drink the bitter liquid and talk about inconsequentials. In the morning, by tacit agreement, they never referred to what had passed during the hours of darkness. There would have been no point.

*When you're up, you're up*, the words of an old nursery rhyme drummed in Stirling's mind. *And when you're down, you're down*.

The letter had been in Stirling's pocket for three days. He took it out, for perhaps the hundredth time, and read it while Melissa fixed breakfast in the cooking alcove of their apartment. It was an official invitation for Mr and Mrs Victor Stirling to visit Administrator Mason Third in his private suite in Government Mile, Boston. The appointed time was three o'clock that afternoon.

Melissa, carrying plates, came into the room. "Victor!"

Stirling put the letter away guiltily. He folded the bed up into the wall, pulled a table leaf out into the same space from another wall, and shook it to release the spring-loaded stools.

"Sorry, honey. I was dreaming again," Stirling said. "But why does he want to see me? What's behind it?"

"Perhaps he wants to say thanks."

"Third would have made Administrator without my help. Anyway, it's been so long, he must be cooking something up."

Melissa set the plates on the table and wrapped her arms

around his chest. "You're tightening up again, Victor. Remember what we agreed? Won't you find out all about it this afternoon?"

Stirling nodded and gratefully buried his face in the black battle-plume of her hair. She had shown a surprising degree of strength in the four months they had been living together in his three-metres-by-three-metres apartment – even when there had been the possibility of a prison sentence. Luckily, the courts had decided that only the Council members who bore arms had been culpable; and none of them had survived the fall. Now that he really knew her, Stirling suspected that Melissa could have handled even a Compression prison; but there were times when her eyes were like those of his mother. Intent, sorrowful, sniper's eyes.

"That's right," he said. "We'll find out all about it this afternoon."

The vac-tube express whisked them to Boston in fifteen claustrophobic minutes, and they walked the rest of the way to Government Mile. Once they were inside the administrative block itself, Stirling presented their two appointment cards to the inspection unit in an elevator car; then they were taken on a five-minute ride which involved several horizontal interchanges. When the car finally stopped and opened its doors, Stirling had no idea how far he had travelled or in what direction. They stepped out into a silver-and-turquoise reception room which was almost spacious, and a door opened automatically in the opposite wall. Beyond it were living quarters, comfortably and informally furnished.

"I hope I look presentable," Melissa said nervously. She was wearing a creation which seemed to consist of light, mist, colour, and very little else.

"You look more than presentable," Stirling replied, "but I'm keeping you to myself just the same. Remember that when you meet our host."

"Oh? You make him sound like someone who would expect *droit de seigneur*."

"It's a bit late for that, isn't it? Let's go in."

Mason Third met them in the doorway. He looked more like a youngish British colonel than ever, but slightly greyer than Stirling had remembered him. He shook hands with them both, retained Melissa's for a beautifully calculated period beyond what was required by convention, ushered them into the long room, and offered drinks. Melissa accepted a glass of synthejuice, and sipped it dutifully.

"Now, Vic. As far as I remember from our first meeting, you're a whisky drinker. Try this."

Stirling tasted malty radiance from a cut glass decanter. "This tastes like . . ."

"Real Scotch," Mason said delightedly. "One of the privileges of office."

His boyish pleasure with one of the trivialities of power was an effective disguise for the real Third, Stirling thought. The speed with which he had reached the top of the political ladder had been equalled by the ruthless energy he had shown on taking office. Thanks to the debacle over Ile 23, the Food Technology Authority's stock had been low when Third was voted in to replace Raddall; and Third had seized his chance to cripple its political machine. Already there were rumours of two attempts on his life, but he still continued on his chosen path as he wielded broadsword and stiletto with equal facility.

Over the second drink, Mason Third said, "I guess we've reached the point where I'm supposed to say, 'I expect you're wondering why I brought you here.'"

Stirling nodded. "I've seen those movies too."

"Here it is then, Vic." Third sat on the edge of his desk. "It hasn't gone before the Chamber of Representatives yet, but I'm scrapping the whole land extension programme. The East Coast has eighteen Iles which cost as much as a defence programme to maintain – and the money can be better used elsewhere."

"I guessed you'd do something like that," Stirling said. "Where do I fit in?"

"This is something that has to be handled just right, Vic. There are a few radical aspects to my proposal, and I'm

171

looking for a good press officer, who will have special responsibilities for seeing to it that the public is kept supplied with the right sort of information." Third twinkled at Stirling over the rim of his glass; obviously he was enjoying himself.

"It doesn't sound like my sort of job." Stirling knew he was being offered a salary perhaps ten times greater than he could earn with the *Record*, but he was unable to feel grateful.

"I disagree. An experienced journalist with first-hand experience of the subject!"

"I've never done any PR work. I'm sorry if that sounds surly, but there it is." Stirling glanced across at Melissa to see how she was reacting. To his surprise, she was sitting bolt upright in her chair, eyes alert.

"Administrator Third," she said quickly. "What are these radical aspects you mentioned? There's nothing very startling in the idea of scrapping the Iles?"

"Nice going," Third said admiringly. "I could offer you a job too."

"She already has one," Stirling cut in.

"I remember something else from our first meeting, Vic. I told you never to go into politics – and that was good advice."

"I'm grateful, but I've no interest in politics. Or public relations work either."

Third got to his feet and lifted a sheaf of photo-prints from his desk. "All right, Vic. I've been indulging myself in a little cat-and-mouse with you. Let's talk seriously now. Before you start making your mind up about this job, let me tell you something about it. Okay?"

"Okay." Stirling felt uncomfortably like a schoolboy being mollified by a clever teacher.

"Fine." Third handed him a grainy, high-magnification print showing hundreds of irregular blotches. "Do you know what that is?"

"Virus? Bacteria?"

"You're on the right track. This micro-organism is a specially developed strain of the blue-green Nostoc algae. It doesn't look like much, but that little fellow is a world champion."

172

"What at?"

"Well – to put it in a rather large nutshell – it's a photosynthetic, nitrogen-fixing, oxygen-evolving, temperature-resistant, aerial micro-organism. Nano-engineering at its best. And it has to be a world-beater – because that's the job we intend it to do for us on Venus."

"Venus!"

"Yes, you've heard of the place, haven't you?"

"I'm sorry. Go on!"

"The trouble with Venus is its greenhouse effect: too much carbon dioxide in the atmosphere. The sun's infra-red waves get in, are modified by the carbon dioxide, can't get out again; and the heat builds up, making the planet unsuitable for human life. That's bad, but one answer we have come up with, is to reduce the carbon dioxide by photosynthesis. And the only way to achieve this is by seeding the atmosphere with a fairly permanent aerial population.

"We – my scientific team, that is – believe that Nostoc R here is the ideal first colonist. He is small enough to remain aloft in the Venusian atmosphere almost indefinitely; he can stand three hundred degrees Centigrade; he can keep himself alive by fixing free nitrogen; and he produces oxygen like mad.

"If we can successfully dust Venus with large quantities of Nostoc R, the outcome will be a fall in the carbon dioxide ratio, a lessening of the greenhouse effect, and a lowering of the surface temperature. Provided we do it on a massive scale, it won't be too long before the surface temperature drops below the boiling point of water. Next there would be rain, the accumulation of a few inches of surface water, a further drop in temperature, and . . .

"Need I say any more?"

"Yes." Stirling's heart was pounding slowly and strongly. "You started off to tell me what you plan to do about the Iles, and you didn't do it. Or did you?"

"You know I did, Vic." Third handed Stirling another photograph. "Your brother had the germ of an idea when he suggested taking Ile 23 to the Moon. Those floating anachronisms have a future ahead of them as factories for the production of Nostoc algae.

"I'll get them to Venus somehow – that part is comparatively easy – but I need people to run them once they're in orbit. A special kind of people. Men and women who could live on the edge of space, Vic, right up there on the edge of space . . ."

Stirling glanced at Melissa – her eyes were luminous with tears, shining like twin planets – and the whole weight of the Compression lifted off him.

"About this job of press officer," he said slowly. "Where would my office be?"

"Take your pick," Third replied. "I've got eighteen Iles, and you can have first choice of orbit, too. I should warn you, though, that this is a long-term project. There'll be no colonisation of the planet in our lifetimes. You'd be getting your mail forwarded to Venus for the rest of your lives."

"What do you think, Melissa?" Stirling touched her fingers with his. "Venus."

She looked at him without speaking, and he knew what she was thinking.

*I always think a good address is* so *important, don't you?*